G000097516

Winter Bayou

Winter Bayou

Kelly Sullivan

the lilliput press
dublin

First published 2 0 0 4 by
THE LILLIPUT PRESS
62–6 3 Sitric Road, Arbour Hill,
Dublin 7, Ireland
www.lilliputpress.ie

A CIP record for this title is available from
The British Library.

ISBN 1 84351 046 4

1 2 3 4 5 6 7 8 9 10

The Lilliput Press receives financial assistance from
An Chomhairle Ealaíon / The Arts Council of Ireland.

Set in 1 2 pt on 1 6 pt Perpetua
Printed by ßetaprint, Clonshaugh, Dublin

for my parents
and for PR

What reasons do you have for despair.
Only one, this sense of emptiness.
José Saramago

18 August 1969, 5 pm
Wright Residence, Slidell, Louisiana

They told us to evacuate but Charlie said there wasn't any need, he said, *it can't get past St Bernard anyhow* and what could I tell him? We were watching the news, the picture getting fuzzy every few minutes like waves and I asked him again if we could leave, *no need, Grace,* he says and I listen to the anchorman tell us again, the New Orleans station, *Everyone within coastal, Chinchuba to Biloxi Bay, should head inland.* The phone rings and I think it's my mother wanting to know if we're leaving, but Charlie answers and laughs so I know it can't be Mother.

5:47 pm

Charlie tells me again this will be great fun, that I should do my hair, look my best, that Sutpen has an apartment right on the water and we'll watch the whole thing and anyway, there'll be other women there, *you'll have a great time, great fun, it'll be great fun.*

Hurricane Camille

Saffir–Simpson Category 5 storm makes landfall shortly before midnight in the Bay St Louis area. The eye of the hurricane measures 12 miles in diameter, with wind speeds estimated upwards of 220 miles per hour, and pressure at 26.85 inches. Damage estimates range from 1 million to 1.5 million dollars, and deaths total 261, with an additional 300 persons reported missing.

Charlie eases the bumper of the Dart up close to the bumper of the Cadillac ahead of us, impatiently smashing his fist into the steering wheel. The water of Bay St Louis eases up closer and closer to the sides of the highway. I look out, cars in both lanes, slow moving to 49 in Gulfport, north to Hattiesburg, away from the rising waters that boil to steel under the sky, maddening in the south.

He pushes up against the bumper once more, forcing him faster across the highway bridge, moving us away from the bay and closer to Pass Christian, Sutpen's apartment, parties, women. The water rises, eases up over the sides of the highway and we continue.

8:16 pm
Hurricane Party at 24 Richelieu Beachfront Apartments,
Pass Christian, Mississippi, home of Sutpen Winters

Used to call Richelieu the Rice Fields no wonder why, flat as a winter bayou and just as wet.

9:37 pm

Count 29 people here, 29 people drinking vodka tonics and dancing to a stereo hi-fi, look out to the parking lot, only vehicles are these, palm trees ripping sideways in the wind and a rain wants to come. I know he's got his arm around some girl, picked which one before he did, platinum blonde like a box of Revlon and styled so tight even this hurricane won't move it. Same for her dress, except he will.

Sliding glass doors open onto a back patio, six floors up, and I press my nose against them, my skin like snail, smooth, flattened, displaced. On the horizon the sky turns mustard and looks like three angry knots of twine, rolling against the water. I call to Charlie crouched next to her on the arm of the chair. He doesn't look up.

258 deaths, American
3 deaths, Cuban
68 missing
8000 deaths, cattle, mostly drownings
5662 homes destroyed
1082 mobile homes destroyed
1 large diesel fuel barge lifted from the harbour, deposited on the median strip between east- and westbound lanes of Highway 90.

11:16 pm

The water's rising almost to the bottom apartments and I call to Charlie, *Charlie*, call him over and over till he answers, *back room*, I swing open the door to darkness, shapes everywhere and I recognize coats, then two bodies, his, the blonde's, *Charlie, we're leaving.* And him, *but love I've just started here, just begun,* kisses her giggling oyster mouth again, another couple bursts in, hands and her legs in pumps pushing me against the doorframe, *get out of here*, they yell, *we're gonna die here*, and he hears them, doesn't hear me, but catches the fear in the other woman's voice and pulls his blonde off the bed, *come on girl, which one's your coat?* and I find my own and run down the stairs, listening to the moan of the palm trees as they hit the ground.

Water, opaque, coffee brown, thick with mud from Lake Pontchartrain, from Lake Borgne, thick with sand and mud from the Intracoastal waterway, from the Chandeleur Sound, thick with mud and silt from the Breton Sound, from the Mississippi River Delta, thick with mud and silt and storm from the Atlantic Ocean pressed frantically against the lowest boards of the jaune three-storey with the wraparound porch, the paint already chipped and fading where the sun hit most frequently, now pounded, again and again by waves, waves higher with each pulse. The water licked over the planks of the porch, ripping them with each return, and forcing them up with each surge. The water reached the windowpanes, pressed against the dark glass, slammed against the wide oak door, pressed harder with each pulse, and continued, a breathing animal against the land. The windows gave way first, then the door burst in, the water rushing and not returning to sea, drowning the oriental rugs, the furniture, the fisherman's chair, chased into the kitchen, sucked out the microwave, the heavy refrigerator, pulled pickles, grape jelly, carrots, half a turkey, twelve Coors cans, a pitcher emptied, threw them about the house. It rushed down hallways and tore down the stairwell, pressed higher and climbed stairs, threw beds, mirrors, shampoo, ivory soap dishes, the pale pages of a book, a violin emptied from its case.

11:22 pm
Richelieu Beachfront Apartments

I hold onto the handle of the car until they come from the apartment complex, tripping and laughing and she pulls a fur coat across her shoulders but doesn't bother to put her arms in the sleeves, *hurry up, Charlie*, and they bend into the wind, her hair lifts and he lifts her skirt, laughter, and they come closer and his hands search her thighs, search her breasts, press her against the car and press into her sides, her back, search his pockets for his keys, *hurry up, Charlie!* he aims drunkenly for the lock, misses, stabs again, the wind picks up her hair again, picks up the lapels of his dinner jacket and blows them near his face, bent in concentration over the lock, her hands in his hair, her lips on his ear. *Hurry up, Charlie!* he pulls the door into the wind, the blonde laughs, falls into the back, and I open the passenger side and slam it, out of the wind. I watch the palm trees blow sideways, grace the sidewalk and dance back up again, over and over, the mustard sky rising in the south and the knots curling and curling against the waves.

Route 49, De Soto National Forest, Mississippi

The trees whip by and the rain whips down and in the back seat she whips her arms like a seizure, uncertain where she is, or why, and then goes suddenly quiet. Charlie drives quickly, speeds over the drifting sand, over the silty water that drifts up from the marshes, that puddles from the rain.

Turns on 26, he stops the car in Wiggins at a motel, and I hurry out next to him, holding my collar up against the driving rain and calling his name. He trips, but catches himself against the door to the office, and I catch up and walk in next to him. Small talk with the attendant, he asks for a room and when he signs the papers, his left hand is naked and wet.

575 miles of roads cleared
30–59 tons of bedding delivered
40,000 textbooks donated from New York schools
30 unclaimed bodies processed by the FBI
infestation of fireants
24 dead at a hurricane party at Richelieu Beachfront Apartments, Pass Christian, Mississippi, after a storm surge 19 feet above the high-tide line, high winds and the knot of hurricane passed through the beachfront Rice Fields and razed the building. Flatter than a winter bayou.

We pull up at the house, so many days later and I wonder if there's any reason to return, or whether we've been ripped apart too, like the house, shredded and pushed past our boundaries, ready only to return to the earth and rise again, different. But he gets out of the Dart and looks at me through the windshield, then motions, gently, like he would if he were touching me early in the morning, when he's still himself.

The front door's blown open and the insides look like they've bled all over the porch, even spilled out into the yard. Beside the forsythia bushes I find the portfolios of photographs from the first year in Philadelphia. There's Thomas's baby picture, black-and-white now indiscernible, muddied, curled and washed like the Louisiana landscape through the windshield of the Dart driving back down here: liquid, trembling. In the front hall he finds his reading glasses folded and unscratched in the middle of the table as if he'd set them there before locking the front door for the night. On the floor, the lampshade and thousands of pieces of glass, some window, some china, some patterned with blue vines curling and curling across the waterlogged pillows, the paperweight, my great-grandmother's wedding dress, a cracked picture frame, three oranges, a limp piece of sheet music.

Charlie reaches down for one of the oranges, brings it close to his face, breathes deeply, then begins to peel it, tossing the fractured shell back onto the floor with the rest. *Grace.* He looks at me, and just so the light from the broken back windows cuts across the hall and he is, new, sharp. *Grace ... I'm gonna leave.* He looks again at my face, but only for a moment, then steps away, pushing another section of orange into his mouth and spitting a seed violently toward the wall.

Upstairs, the damage is no less. In the hall I step over emptied drawers and spilled bottles of cold cream, across the wide arc of pale grey mascara flung against the hardwood floor, itself warped and discoloured. I walk past my son's room, past our bedroom, walk toward the blue room. The door hangs crookedly, ripped from its top hinges. Inside is a sea of sheet music, sharps, whole notes, pizzicatos piled as if for a bonfire, but still wet and already with a faint scent of decay. I dig my hands into the pile, pull up the cream pillows from the couch, drag their heavy forms out and fling them, drowned bodies onto sand. I pull at the drapes from the smashed windows, their folds dripping and twisting together and there, under the weight of indigo cloth, is the violin.

Its body, waterlogged and darkened, feels unnaturally heavy. I lift it by its neck, but quickly slide a hand down to the ribs and hold it with my fingers on either side of the end button. Water dribbles from the f-holes when I tilt it forward. The strings hang uselessly, their ends unravelling and sharp. The tailpiece dangles from the G-string. Two dulled spots in the spruce belly mark where the bridge used to rest. I turn it over in my hands and run a finger along the thin crack that arches through the maple back from the fingerboard all the way to the base. There is a looseness inside its body, a dull tap when I turn it from side to side. The wood, heavy with the water, is cold in my hands. *Grace!* I hear his anger and when I rise my knees are wet from kneeling in the rubble.

When I rose, my knees were cold and stinging from the cold snow that lined the top of the pond and the surrounding trees, contrasting the dark, wet of their branches with the shocking smoothness of the iced surface. I stood from the bank where I'd leaned, looking out across the expanse. I reached down for the violin case and took a tentative step onto the glassy surface. My saddle shoes had slick soles that slid before I found my balance with each step. Skirts blew around my ankles, tightened there, making it even more difficult to step forward into the space that only cold could inhabit. After thirty uncertain paces I stopped, looked up. An entire forest around me and then a space no one had ever occupied before, my space, the centre where each flux of water from Ridley Creek pulsed and widened, where the motion that smoothed the beaches and carved the edges of the lake began. I looked up to the chilled empty sky, my hair against my body, my dress pressing the shape of my hips, breasts just coming clear under the layers of wool and velvet.

I knelt next to the case and snapped open the catches, the sound loud and unnatural in the dead landscape. I pulled the instrument awkwardly from the felt-lined box and tightened the bow. I raised the violin to my shoulder and pressed down my chin. Light flashed on wood, the sharp contrast of the grained and polished instrument against the dull black lines of branches, trunks, the snow in collars against their bases. I touched the bow to the strings, an uncertain sound that whined into the space I'd owned, that whined, then wailed, then sang uncertainly, each stroke of the bow too short for a full breath, each note muttered and lost into space, separate from me, this wood and gut and ebony between us.

Grace, I turned quickly from the blue room, still holding the ruined violin by its neck and silencing the clanging tailpiece with my opposite hand. I stepped through the hallway, down the stairs, stood in the entrance to the living-room where he stood in front of the fireplace, stood in front of it dropping the short flames of match after match into the wet mouth and watching them go out in thin lines of smoke. *Grace!* and he turned, saw me in the doorway, saw the violin, and softened again, paused mid-strike, then continued, his eyes on the burst of flame that rose and levelled, on its long flight to the dark wet mouth, on the brief glow of red in the tip after it burnt out. *Grace I ...* he looked up again, but not at me, at the mangled and darkened instrument, *Grace ... I'm sorry about all of this and I'm going to help you straighten up and then I'm going.*

So I was right, we are washed past boundaries, cannot go back.

First time with Charlie I was seventeen. 1943 I guess, but I don't remember it. Not a thing of it, though later, in '44 and '45, we went up Ridley Creek every weekend, just walked right up it, through the park, through the deeper woods. I'd tell him we'd get shot, like deer, our hides shadow in the shadows. He laughed, *deer don't walk up creeks, Grace, don't you know anything? Fox walk up creeks. We'd better listen for horses*, he laughed again. Foxhunters, bay horses steaming and blowing steam, their necks dark with sweat, crimson-coated riders without faces, the sound of hooves, no sound when I looked up, then the sound of hooves again. Each time we lay down together, I thought of pounding fetlocks, the flex of tendons, the press of horseshoe against my chest, the ring of purple flesh it would leave on my stomach, his galloping, galloping into me.

After, I'd shut the door quietly and walk around the creaking floorboards and to my room, feel in the dark for its case and take the violin back out into the night. In summer I walked back up the creek again, the water numbing my bare feet, in winter, walked to the middle of the pond. Each night, after, I filled the space we'd made with the whine and later the voice of the violin, my voice, coming quicker and quicker, my fingers finding the notes through his hair, quicker and quicker through my bow arm sweeping across the strings, down the flutes of muscle on his back. It came mellow and low then quicker and harder and pizzicato and striking each note, forcing it from the wood and into the still sycamores, pin oaks, maples.

Always, the violin called between the spaces.

9 weeks cleaning

12 plates of glass from Baton Rouge

356 shingles, replaced

7478 dollars, total repairs

Salvaged:

3 queen beds, no mattresses

set of 6 camel-back chairs, water-stained, rose in colour

dining-room table, wood darkened in waves

6 paintings, hung high

Charlie's eyeglasses

The Poetics of Music in the Form of Six Lessons, Igor Stravinsky, Cambridge, Harvard University Press, 1942. Jammed behind the plumbing under the counter in the upstairs bathroom to hold a warped pipe. Dry next to running water.

He called the refuse company on a Monday, 3:45 pm. An hour later they came, removed the three dumpsters in the back yard. Now three brown rectangles, grass dead where they waited so long, holding photographs, linens, flower pots, typewriter, Concerto in A minor, A. Vivaldi.

At 5:45 pm he opens the trunk of the Dart and lifts in the two suitcases we own. Inside, pressed white shirts, three pairs of grey pin-stripe pants, underwear. In his pocket, a billfold. I stand on the porch, lean against a post and breathe deeply the scent of waterlogged and rotting wood. He walks around the car to the driver's side and puts his key in the lock, turns it, his left hand on the handle. He looks up at me and opens the door, presses his hat down and waits there, door open, sweat dripping down the sides of his face from November in Louisiana. *I'll come back. Sometime. I'll … send you some money.* I face him, leaning and breathing in the scent of afternoon heat burning the wood even as it rots, heat warming my hair, pulled back sharp in the afternoon sun. *I'll give you money … for the violin. Get it repaired, I'll send you money.* I lean, breathe the rotting wood, then pick a shard from the pole and split it, over and over to soft dust, damp in my hands. *I'll.* He adjusts his hat again. *I'll call.* He gets into the Dart and I drop the wood from my hands, push my warmed hair from my face and think I can smell him there, smell him from this morning when he was himself, touching me softly awake and climbing my body, softly.

He never did want to own me.

Three weeks later the papers come in the mail. *St Tammany County Justice official intention to divorce.* Underneath, the neat white envelope from Clair Brothers Violin Makers. *Ms Wright: We have begun repairs on your violin. We advise that cost of restoration far exceeds the value of the instrument. Until further instruction, however, we willingly continue as requested.*

Purchased: 1894, Sears and Roebuck Catalog mail order. *Violin complete with bow, strings, rosin, case and instructions, $42.50,* the most expensive model to date.

Delivered: Thomas Selverin Worcester, 46 County Road #2, Sycamore Mills, Pennsylvania. Opened upon arrival and played.

Born: To Thomas Selverin Worcester and Grace Freemont Worcester: Robert Thomas Worcester, 1895, to the sound of his father's fiddling; Joshua Benson Worcester, 1899, to the sound of his mother's strained singing; David Freemont Worcester, 1900, to the sound of his brother's screams.

Raised: In Sycamore Mills, Pennsylvania on the 200-acre dairy farm to the sound of cattle lowing, to the rush of Ridley Creek, to the voice of a violin until

Killed: In 1919 by a bad heart, Thomas Selverin Worcester silenced the instrument, and his youngest son, David, for nearly four years.

Born: To David Freemont Worcester, no longer mute, and Juliana Harford Worcester: Thomas David Worcester, 1925, to the sound of rain; Grace Elizabeth Worcester, 1926, to the sound of Vivaldi Concerto #6 in A minor on the new Atwater Kent radio, static-filled and sweet.

Delivered: To Grace Worcester on the event of her birthday, 1936, the violin, opened and played upon arrival and complete with newly

Purchased: strings, Pirastro Tonica $3.50/set, and case, synthetic leather, felt interior with room for two bows and storage for rosin, strings, and mute, $27.85.

*L*esson *O*ne

To explain——or, in French, to explicate, from the Latin explicare, to unfold, to develop——is to describe something, to discover its genesis, to note the relationship of things to each other, to seek to throw light upon them.

Igor Stravinsky
The Poetics of Music in the Form of Six Lessons

6 April 1947

The Philadelphia Enquirer

photograph: CHARLES WRIGHT and GRACE WORCESTER
Charles Wright of Philadelphia and Grace Worcester of
Sycamore Mills, Delaware Co., to be married this Saturday,
April 8 at 2 pm at St Peter's Episcopal Church, Philadelphia.
The couple will reside in the city where Mr Wright holds
employment as a railroad foreman for the Philadelphia Trans-
portation Company.

Charlie came home crazed *like bullets, Grace, like bullets on two tracks, like thoroughbred bullets* with the new President's Conference Committee cars, 100 from the St Louis Car Company, 85 to Germantown Depot, Route 23, Charlie's line. *Gotta ride one, Grace, like a thoroughbred, call 'em streamlined,* replaced the 1912 Brill-built Nearside cars. *Like 85 thoroughbred bullets, quiet and lightning fast,* foxhunters, thoroughbreds' heavy breath, two wicks steaming from their nostrils, their metallic hooves heavy as bullets, pounding through the woods, galloping across my chest, the sound of hounds baying and the far-off cant of fox.

Waited till tomorrow to tell him I could feel the child steaming inside me; doctor said so, too.

When he did sit down and listen it was just evening, 8:15 perhaps, just evening and I'd just put down the violin when I heard his keys in the lock. Stopped just in time, loosened the bow, the horsehair suddenly slack, dull. When I came into the kitchen, small as a closet in the farmhouse back home, he was already loosening his bootlaces, and I told him, his face suddenly slack, dull. *A child.* He pulled off the left boot, the oil and clay from the tracks falling around it. He looked up at me. *A child already, Grace?* As if I could have stopped him, always hunting onward. I knew it wasn't so, but I could feel its firm feet and fine toes kick out against my body, kick out and catch me so I sucked in my breath. *Yes, Charlie. Already.* He dropped the second boot and worked the muscles in his foot with his callused and lined hands, the kitchen light catching on his ring and flashing across my face, across the fading squares of light on the white kitchen walls. I touched a hand through my hair and he stood, reached out to my hip and touched, softly touched, my stretch of stomach. *So when, then?* He moved his hands up my sides and over my breasts and across the taut cords of my neck, his thumbs pressing my cheeks taut, his lips pressed against my lips, my body taut against his. My fingers moved through his hair, down his back, and when he drew away I said, *February sometime, a while*, and pressed loose strands of hair from my mouth with my fingers that press down the strings, the gut and fibre and the Pernambuco bow.

The year in Philadelphia was gentle and close to childhood. The violin lessons came soon after I told him about our baby. His keys in the lock again, and my fingers still on the strings, the bow pulling low chords, choked chords. He stepped in and listened; then I saw him. *Charlie!* My fingers whipped back from the instrument as away from heat, its heat real and resonating even after I'd lowered the bow to my side and tightened my jaw, stood next to the music stand, the sheets of paper pale and marked in the coming darkness. *So you do play it.* He stepped into the room and I shrank back, moving the violin to the felt-lined case, its wood delicate and thin under my fingers stroking the spruce belly. *Grace, play for me*, he moved to me and touched my elbow as I slid the bow into its holders and lowered the lid. He caught the top halfway closed, *play something for me*. I pulled back my elbow and shrank away from him, the scent of the violin, the rosin in the air, floating around us and slowly falling upon our shoulders, our hair, our shoes. *Charlie, your shoes!* I pushed him off of the crimson oriental carpet, wedding gift from his parents, pushed him back to the linoleum, his footsteps like hoofbeats, regular, cadenced, backward from my fingers gentle and now teasing against his chest, and my lips, teasing now against his lips, forgetting the rosewood, maple, the spruce of the violin, forgetting the rosin that still rose and fell with our motion and breath in the falling square of light and evening.

He pulled out a cane-backed kitchen chair and loosened his boots and I opened the door to the oven, the heat real and pushing into me in waves. *Do you want some lessons?* I reached to the foil inside and pulled back a corner, prodding the meat, smelling it. *Lessons? Is my cooking that bad, Charlie?* I laughed and he rose and smiled and rose to me, his hand around my waist over the oven, the heat still rising in waves, pressing against both of us and forcing us back, *of course not, but the violin. Do you want lessons with the violin?* The oven shut and I turned to him, my jaw tight and tense to his gaze. He smiled again and passed a hand over my stomach. *Not because you need them, Grace.* He stared hard for a second, *though I wouldn't know*, and softened, *but because you're gonna be here a lot, not gonna go a lot of places with this baby, you know?* He moved away from me and sat back at the table. *You might as well have some lessons, something to do during the day before I get home.*

And so the next day I found someone, called and walked there, the violin rocking in its case.

I walk up the stairs, imagine the shift of a violin rocking, rocking if I could carry it upstairs, could unclasp the case and lift it from the felt lining, could tighten the bow and bring it to my chin. I walk to the blue room, look out the window, look past the drapes, no longer indigo, but white, and light, fluttering like wings, uncertain of where to land.

I walk outside again, walk down the drive and follow the broken poles where the power lines once hung before being ripped away with the wind and water, washed like eels, unfurling in the waves. The music begins slowly, a soft refrain, but I silence it and in the silence comes his face, the glance down, the turn of my body away from his body, the change; I think of this and feel a rise in my throat and walk more quickly, into Slidell, stand at the bus stop and think of his hands gripping the wall along the Mississippi, the barges on the water heavy with machinery and rust, our voices, our lack of voice. I climb up the steps of the bus, ride down Fremeaux Avenue, down Montrose, ride up the ramp to Route 11, ride across the flat expanse of Lake Pontchartrain and watch the grey water, still and reflecting the still sky, its cloud cover, the hint of rain.

Settlement Music School, 416 Queen Street, Philadelphia

Charlie's friend Manny said this is the place for music instruction, says, *my boy goes here, plays his violin here every day and you should hear him, my boy.* He should know, too, they say his boy's the most talented player in the city, Brazilian, adopted, blind in both eyes and plays and plays and plays, listening, and cannot know who's listening, or how. Twelve kids, total, all adopted, none quite right.

A tall suited man with a thin, elegant moustache opens his office door and motions me to enter, introduces himself, *MrsWright, I am Johann Grolle, I am most pleased to make your acquaintance*, his accent heavily Dutch, he takes my hand gently, as if I were a child. In his office, a print of Picasso's *Portrait of Igor Stravinsky*; a black-and-white photograph of a dark-haired man bowing intensely; five violin cases resting on all the available chairs, two opened, the instruments glistening in afternoon sunlight. He reaches for the one of mahogany, lifts it by its neck and plays a scale, up and up, first to third to fifth position, fingers long and wrist arched. He looks at me. *We would like to hear you play, MrsWright.This is not a test.* He smiles, his foreign face relaxing, plays again, a progression of chords, up and up and up. *We need to know your level of necessary instruction*, he motions for me to put down my case and take out the violin. *Please, do not be shy. I only listen.* Again, his smile.

I set the case down on his desk and take out the violin, the maple wood pale in the sudden light through the window.

Outside, a courtyard with children throwing a white ball and laughing, though there is no sound through the thick pane of the window, only their motion, their mouths wide, hair racing back from their faces and their feet slapping the pavement. I tighten the bow, bring the violin between my chin and my collarbone. He nods to me, smiles. *Go ahead, Mrs Wright. This is not a test. I will only be listening.* The first notes come tentative, halting, then more freely. He moves a closed case from a chair and sits, looks out the window at the children, their shadows playing across the room, across my violin, across my face. He watches them and the notes come more quickly, the bow moving long and low across the strings, the voice low, then higher, moaning, then aching to reach the children outside, to fill their opened and empty mouths, to match their footsteps, their arms winging the white ball into air. He only listens, and so I play on; he does not want to take my music and make it something of his, as I know Charlie would, he only listens as he's listened so many other times, his eyes on the children, marking each note in cadence with the movement of calf muscles, with the stretch of their lips in a shout. He closes his eyes, leans back in the chair and I strike the last note.

His eyes open once again and he turns away from the children and looks at me. *Thank you, Mrs Wright.* I lower the violin to my side, *that's the first I've played for anyone.* He looks on, *yes, well thank you, you can come again tomorrow for your first lesson, Mrs Wright, you will learn with Mr Edgar Ortenberg, this is intermediate classes, Mrs Wright, I think you will find them suitable to your playing.* He stands up, tall and sudden through the light coming in from the window, the children dancing shadows across his back, and when he leans over his desk, across his face. He lifts my violin case, finds a pen and a sheet of white paper and writes *Edgar Ortenberg, 3:20 pm Wednesday*, hands this to me. *Thank you, Mr Grolle,* I put the violin away, click shut the clasps and lift it to my side, look at him, again, and he smiles.

7 June 1947
Philadelphia

Charlie comes home again excited, *these cars, Grace!* and I smile and touch his hair when I pass to the oven, the meat cooking there, losing its red. *When are you gonna see 'em, these bullet cars!* Each day I listen to this, he unlaces his boots, the oil and clay littering the linoleum around them. I open the oven and the waves of heat push against me, *if you want me to stop by some time I will, Charlie.* I pull the roast from the oven, the scent of potatoes and onions thick in the evening air. *I'd like to.* He puts a hand on my stomach before I cut the meat, feels the small arch of stomach and drops his hands to the silverware, grasps a knife and waits for me to slice the roast and pass him the flesh.

Only in morning will he enter me, his hands waking with a gentle circular stroke across my inner thigh, across my stomach, over my breasts, circling each and softly stroking my collarbone, the cords of my neck, stroking softly my cheek. He wakes me, softly touching the smooth flesh of my inner arm, working his fingers down to my fingers, their worked tips, handling them, bringing them to his mouth and moving onto me, softly, like waking, his weight across my hips and then moving, a soft canter then moving, like thoroughbreds hunting early morning, the mist rising off the fields, their hides taut in the morning light and their breath coming quicker and quicker, and farther, the fox, moving upstream, then galloping, the hooves pounding and pounding the soft earth, cleaving grass from soil, marking in patterns, galloping and then reaching the first fence and rising

36

off muscular quarters, their hooves lifting together in air and tightening together in air, body suddenly free and light in air, neck stretched and hindquarters lifted from the earth into air and floating across the brush and ditch and floating lower and lower and touching down, softly loosed back to earth, and softly touching my stomach, my lips with his fingertips, then his lips, touching my neck, and dropping his head to my collar-bone, softly, body landing.

Ortenberg says, *take your desire for a full sound from your fingers and move it into your bow, swing it wild to fling out your name.* I watch him watch me, catch his eyes catch the flock of school-children playing ball outside and I can play, wide, swinging the bow, catch my rhythm, my mouth, my tongue, only when he watches them. Inside my child turns and I can feel his kick, play louder against the movement.

Ortenberg looks close at the violin as I play and then says, *did you ever play this instrument outside?* He pulls it gently from my hands, turns it like a piece of fruit examined for bruises. I run a hand down the bulge of my stomach, feeling ripe. *Yes.* The trees' thin shapes lined with snow, the frozen water stretching before me, the violin going cold in my hands.

Ortenberg says, *see here, this small line?* His long fingers whisper over the instrument, his fingernail runs near a fracture the width of a hair, from the bottom of an f-hole. *This is from outside. You cannot take a violin outside to play.* He turns it again in his hands, this time looking at me and touching the maple and spruce like a small object kept only for movement, never for sound. *You see, wood has an affinity for moisture. If you let it become dry, as I see you have, this is by going outside in cold weather, say in the snow, as you may have, yes?* The space I had to fill with sound, with my sound to stop his galloping through a silenced landscape. *This allows the wood to shrink, to remove the moisture is to minimize the wood, you see, to shrink and make it brittle, to make it subject to tensions it cannot bear. Yes?* The movement of my bow hand, back and forth through the cold, pulling sound from the strings, making the trees, the red maple, the pin oak, the sycamore, bear a sound. *Wood likes moisture of, say, 55%. This is ideal. And lack of humidity causes these cracks, like this one, and these cause the playing to be less, see? The crack comes because the glue does not allow the seams, where the plates meet the ribs, to open. The tension is too much.* He turns the pegs so that the strings release all tension and fall away from the bridge, then hands me the violin. His face relaxes to a smile. *But it is alright, Mrs Wright. We fix this easily.* He goes to his desk and writes on a slip of paper. The violin is warm from his hands. *Take it to them and they will fix it for you, and when it is done, we will begin again, yes?* I look at the scrap of paper. *Clair Brothers Violin Makers, 22 Moore Street.*

Lake Pontchartrain, endless and frozen, the trees overhead creaking like violin strings in the sudden cold of night, of snow, and the snow, falling slowly, falling across my shoulders, across my face, falling across my bow and weighing it, making each note shorter, strained, halted. I look across the lake, the endless water reflecting, the lack of movement, ride to Route 11 in New Orleans, to St Bernard Avenue, to North Rampart Street, to the corner of Esplanade where it stops and I step off into the heat of the city, the humidity, to the French Quarter, to Bourbon Street and up to Decatur, to the French Market, to the Mississippi River.

I lean against the wall and listen to the slap of the river underneath the walkway, look across the rich coloured water and watch the barges pull gears, teeth rusted and broken, from St Bernard, from the gas factories, upstream. I look across to the streets spreading slowly from the opposite bank, the roofs catching sunlight, the row upon row of houses, the places I will never go.

Charlie moves carefully over my stomach, still small so early. He brushes my hair away from my face, wakes me quietly with his desire, and we are quiet in the pale sunlight of summer morning. The sheets are cool before the heat and we come closer with the cool, with snow on sycamore branches, the muffled pond, the empty space of white sheets, folding and folding like snow drifts, the air tightening the wood and pulling it, the tension more than it could bear. When closest, we were breaking.

Clair Brothers calls and I take a bus to 22 Moore Street. The receptionist shows me to the back room, the workshop filled with the scent of woods, glue, of heat and moulding. The ceiling is several stories up and windows line the far wall, running from chest height to the roof, three floors. At the far side of the factory a small man motions for me, and the receptionist pushes me toward him. I am careful through the tables, the rows of tools, small and precise, each clean and metal and ordered. At the far side, the man becomes even smaller, reaches only to my shoulder, his apron an unbleached cotton, coloured like resin, in his hands, my violin.

Hello, miss, he is shy and looks at the hue of the violin, newly varnished, reflecting the light from the windows behind us. *You see here, we've repaired the crack so you can't even see it.* The belly ran smoothly from fingerboard past the f-holes, to the end button. No break in the constant grain of the wood. *You see, we had to go inside her to reinforce this.* He leans over his workbench and picks up a small diamond of wood. *We use studs, like this, glued inside along the crack. She's as good as new. Maybe better.* He looks up at me and hands me the violin. *Watch out for humidity in this weather. Keep her someplace dry.* He shoves his hands deep into the pockets of his apron and smiles. *Oh! But not too dry. That's what caused the crack in the first place. See, too much moisture and you're gonna warp her, but too little and you'll have more cracks, and next time might be worse.* He smiles again. I nod, and relax with the smooth grain under my fingers once more. *Thank you.* He nods this time and opens the case for me. I place the instrument, polished and new, against the felt lining and press down the clasps. The man turns away from me and picks up a brush and dustpan, then quickly turns back. *Oh! Just walk straight through and Ms Jepson will settle out with you, alrighty?* I nod, and walk straight through.

Charlie came home talking trains again. *Have you heard, Grace? The Freedom Train!* I stand in front of the oven and shake my head. He walks into the kitchen and sits to take off his boots. The windows are open and an evening city breeze moves the curtains. Inside me I feel the child move with the change in temperature. I move closer to the oven, slowing him back to sleep. *Grace, it's gonna be incredible! A freedom train to drive all over the country, and we're loaning them cars! The PA Railroad loaning them cars! Imagine that! Three exhibit cars, three of our new PCCs and then a baggage from Santa Fe. ALCO's giving them the engine.* He stands and gently moves me away from the oven and stands my silhouette against the bright lowering evening in the window, looks at the bulge of stomach. *How's he doing? Hey, you've gotta come see this train. Comes in September. And Grace, it's starting here in Philly!* He sat back down at the table and outside the sun lowers again, the evening coming cool through the windows and the child moving once more with the change, the violin in the next room, warm in its case.

Settlement Music School, 416 Queen Street, Philadelphia

Ortenberg says, *you're playing better, Mrs Wright, much better. This is perhaps because you play for the baby, eh?* He winks and the child moves in me, and I want to put the violin in its case, close to the felt lining and the snapped clasps, close inside the darkened faux leather, silenced inside. *Or … perhaps you play better because you have been working hard, yes?* He touches my shoulder, says, *it is time, I think, for some theory. This is important as well as the playing. You should read, should understand why to play as much as to play.* He walks to the oak desk at the far side of the room and sunlight cuts through his hair, playing with the chestnut and forcing shadows over his brow. Outside, children run, gesture silently and throw a ball across the macadam court. Their frocks white haze through the window. He pulls open a drawer and brings out a thin book bound in leather. *Igor Stravinsky. The Poetics of Music in the Form of Six Lessons.* He hands me the book.

This song is a train song

Charlie guides me by the elbow through the crowds of people to the locomotive, tells me, *see Grace, it's a diesel engine, not steam. This is the future, Grace.* He reaches toward the gracefully curving metal, touches it like he would touch me. *It's an ALCO PA engine, no need for water at all, just diesel fuel.* I step toward it and touch the red and blue stripes streaking along the sides, hear the big band coming over the loudspeakers and look up again to Charlie, reaching for my elbow, holding my arm and looking then at the bulge of stomach and the kick of child.

It's a song about a train

The voices rise up again, *that paint job's by Chester Mack. You know him, yeah? You've heard of him.* A balloon pops behind me, a voice cries out, sounds rise in crescendo, rise again. The loudspeakers, two budding metal flowers high above the heads of the crowd, roar with the big band.

Where the engineer is Uncle Sam

A woman nearby, *the colours, so lovely,* and another baby cries and a dog runs along the track, darting between legs, the crowd a roar in my ears and Charlie takes my elbow again, leads me down along the metal like a bullet, thin and sleek thoroughbred, galloping, says, *these are our cars, loaned from our railroad. See, they painted 'em, but we'll get them back, after they go all around the country.* The loudspeakers scratch and whistle big band, then slower.

Here comes the freedom train

Bing Crosby and the Andrews Sisters.

Just like a Paul Revere

Smell of roasted peanuts and the seller's yell over the roar of the crowds and the speakers break through.

It's coming into your hometown

The wind picks up my hair and blows voices then whines into the tunnel of the station and Charlie guides me, *Grace, let's go inside, you'll love the inside, upholstered in genuine leather and the President might even stand at the end.* The loudspeakers roar again and a child cries and the dog runs by, the wind whining into the tunnel as we step up inside.

You'd better hurry down
It's coming into your hometown

Say it loud
Riding on the freedom train

L^{esson} *T*^{wo}

*In [the musician's] hands all that I have considered as
not being music will become music. From this I conclude
that tonal elements become music only by virtue of
their being organized, and that such organization
presupposed a conscious human act.*

Igor Stravinsky
The Poetics of Music in the Form of Six Lessons

Settlement Music School, 416 Queen Street, Philadelphia

Ortenberg says, *play this line again. I think you have lost some sense of the sound here.* I pick up the bow and set it down on the strings, pulling from them the sounds, the chords, the trill, the decrescendo to piano, look from the page to the children, huddled together outside, unmoving, silent, and ordered against the dark macadam. The notes muddle, I play a sharp meaning something else, Ortenberg says, *there, see you did the same thing. Play this low. I think perhaps you have lost concentration, Mrs Wright?* The baby kicks against me again, and I feel the unnatural weight when I turn to look at him. Ortenberg looks at me, and I know he has been listening. The children are silent and stilled. My child has been listening. *I think this has been enough, please.* Ortenberg says nothing.

I combed the snow from my hair, braided it in two long, damp whips, picked out a maple twig and broke it, again and again to soft dust, damp in my hands.

I went back out when the first light came violet over the landscape, turning the snow the colour of ash, like ash falling from the burn barrel onto the snow when my dad stoked the trash, the scent of burning paper and wood, creosote and varnish thickening the air and falling thickly, coating the snow. I walked out, the first light guiding me and the first snow falling against the crusted surface of the old, falling slowly as the sunlight shudders through cloud cover early and livid. At the pond, I walked to the centre and opened the violin case against the ice, the cold forcing tension into the strings, making them pop and chirp. I tightened the bow and began to finger as I'd learned when a young child, first and third position, moving slowly up a scale then more quickly through movements, the first progression of a sonatina, the sound filling the space between the trees, moving my bow hand more quickly and pulling the notes, the sound filling the emptiness between birch and beech, between his hands and my back, between our silences. The snow falling harder.

I watched as I played, each flake landing on the varnished surface and beading there, each bead vibrating with the notes I pulled and then running slowly to the edges and gathering along the purfles, then moving to the weak places on the edging and dripping down the ribs, to the curled underbelly. I watched the snow fall harder, watched each flake fall onto the gut strings, hang there, uncertain, then melt to a bead of water and drip to the fingerboard, to the belly. I watched the snow come harder, filling the spaces between the trees, filling with greater silence than I could fill, watched it catch on my bow and melt there, then drip to the horsehair and wash out the colour, the rosin, to translucence. I played until the bow yelped uselessly over the strings, until the snow covered the linseed varnish in white before it could melt, until my fingers were stiff and white, until the landscape came azure in early morning light and silent, emptied by the last moan of wet bow over wet strings. I looked into the spaces, empty of me.

Pennsylvania Railroad's First Diesel Locomotive, East of Sycamore Mills

I feel full of child. The train galloping on iron hooves. *The first diesel locomotive in the state, Grace! And here we are!* He puts his arm around my waist, then as an afterthought, his hand across the bulge of stomach, so full of child, and galloping, the grass underneath my back and he is gentle, less gentle, pulls at the nape of my dress, then gentle again, galloping. *So what do you think?* He smiles at me, and outside the landscape wears a frock of white snow, moves silently, soundless in the courtyard, their bodies in movement without sound, the violin creating sound and marching them, moving them, Ortenberg's eyes following them, then the notes, then my face, the child kicks and the galloping galloping stops. West Chester Station. *Charlie, can we leave now? Grace, one more stop until your parents' place.*

The box is long and thin, and the bow inside Pernambuco, butter-coloured horsehair from Mongolia, mother-of-pearl on the frog and an ivory inlay tip initialled gWe. I play them The Firebird Suite. First sound since the snow, and it fills the room, the snow laying down outside, silently, sound covers the spruce tree, opened boxes underneath.

I wouldn't have known except when he comes home he says to me, *I've found a way to love you, Grace.* He didn't wake me that morning, and doesn't again until after the child is born. In the evening, when he comes close to kiss my neck I lean over the bulge of stomach and oven, I breathe in the scent of roast, search out her scent in the rough lines and calluses of his hands.

At night, after bathing, I stand in front of the fireplace and comb my hair in a fan across my back, comb in front of the flames until each strand, butter-coloured, dries flat. Charlie reads the newspaper and I see him watch, neither owning, nor wanting.

14 February 1948

The Philadelphia Enquirer

THOMAS ANDREW WRIGHT

Son born to Charles Wright and Grace Worcester Wright, 23 Georgia Street, Philadelphia, at 2:55 pm, Thursday. The child is the first for the couple. Charles Wright holds employment as a railroad foreman for the Philadelphia Transportation Company.

After he is born, everything is silenced to me. In morning, I wake to his mouth opening and straining, straining with screams Charlie says he hears, he cannot wake from. The child moves small fists and fingers where the notes and chords have filled, now filtered into late winter sunlight, weak and straining across his wicker rocker and the crimson carpets, slowly fading. The violin and Charlie are both silent and lie still, hushed like twin shells, washed in waves.

Charlie comes home quietly, unlaces his boots and lines them in the alcove of the front door, walks to the child sleeping in the last light of afternoon. *Don't wake him, he's been quiet.* Charlie sits again and tells me flatly that we're moving. *New Orleans. I've got a job there. Managing the public transportation, pays well.* I run my fingers down the ordered panes of glass then pull the curtains shut. When I walk past him I nod, and catch the far-off scent of woman, and of lust.

The wind blows against the door and then catches it and blows it open when I finally lift the latch. Charlie bends over on the opposite side, holding Thomas out of the rain and wind, waiting for me to sit down and take him, his kicking feet, his fleshy hands. The rain pounds on the windshield of the Chrysler, pounds on the windows of our apartment, three stories up, and pounds across the steps of the front porch. The wind picks up, blows the rain sideways and gathers the crumpled papers, the rags and cigarette butts from the street and sends them in a whirlwind at the end of Georgia Street, sends them into greater Philadelphia, into the crowds walking down South Street, into the taxis and traffic, into the rest of the dirt. The rain comes stronger again, and hushes the wind with a steady pounding, pounding. I gather the hem of my dress, pull my cardigan tight across my shoulders with my left hand and yank the door shut with my right. Charlie hands me the baby and I take him even before I can wipe back the wet strands of hair that cling to my forehead and cheeks.

After turning over for a minute, the Chrysler roars louder than the rain and the windshield wipers clear a view of our apartment once more. The rain slows, the wind dances trash down the end of the street, Charlie wheels the car around and we drive, slowly at first through the storm, toward the airport. *Grace, did you forget anything at all? This is it.* Thomas cries. On the back seat, the violin seems suddenly silent, though I haven't played in four months. *I think we have everything.* He moves uncertainly for my knee, places his rough, work-stained hand there and then removes it, just as awkwardly. I adjust the blankets around Thomas, moving the wet edges away from his face and his fists. He cries louder. *Well, we're off.*

Charlie drops us off under the awning at the Philadelphia International Airport and comes back, running through the rain, his suit an old three-piece from my father, darker brown over the shoulders and arms where the rain soaks it. Under the awning he shakes water from his head like a dog. He smiles. He cannot stop smiling. Once again, he takes Thomas from me and I adjust my bag over my arm and smooth down my dress where the small body rumpled it. At the check-in counter, Charlie reaches into his breast pocket for my ticket. After, we walk to the side, away from the lines of people that move steadily, like rain, blown sideways only by a baggage carrier with a full cart. Charlie says, *you'll be alright. Get a taxi when you're in New Orleans, and stay at the Friendship Inn, Slidell. Ok? It's already paid for, all taken care of, ok? I'll be there tomorrow night. Wait for me there. I'll be there, ok?* Charlie touches Thomas on the top of his head and he cries again, and then he touches my cheek, more today than he has in months, touches me softly and he pauses, just for a moment pauses and I know he's thinking about me, how I feel about all of this despite his excitement, and then he's gone again, back inside himself and I walk toward the aircraft alone once more, think of him driving the Chrysler Town and Country to Louisiana, think of the woman he will visit before he leaves and the way he will pause for her then take her, the way she will let him; think of the violin, silent and still on the back seat.

We pull into the long dirt drive, lined on either side by trenches thick with mint-green algae. The air is heavy with the scent of moisture, rot, and heat. Overhead, cypress trees arch and meet. I hold Thomas in my lap and Charlie tells me again and again that he's not seen the place, *but Mellot found it and says it's great, we'll love it.*

The road weaves and I lean out the open window, look for alligators in the green water along the sides. Then, on the right, the house, white turning grey, fading into the bayou, leans into the thin line of cypress trees. Charlie turns the Town and Country into the lawn in front of the house when the road ends abruptly at a chicken-wire fence on rotting posts. I step out of the car into the still air, and Charlie comes around to take the baby. I run my fingers through my hair and we walk toward the front porch, both silent in the Louisiana heat. The house, raised off the ground, has a sagging wraparound porch with white portico columns and waterlogged canvas blinds running between each one to keep out the rain and rot. A single-storey wing extends from the left, and the roof is patched and irregular. On the right, a chimney rises, and rust from the gutters runs in stains for several feet down the front of the house.

Charlie steps across the front lawn, half clover half dead, and walks up the steps to the porch. He opens the screen door, and fits his key in the lock, balancing the baby on his left arm. I walk up behind him and run my hands down the rough wood porticos. The sunlight, blocked by the canvas shades, cannot reach inside the porch and it's cooler in the darkness. Charlie stops in front of the strangely official oak front door and waits for me to step next to him. He puts his free hand around my waist, then leans in to kiss me. I kiss back, the heat crouching outside the porch, Charlie's hand moving to the back of my head, his fingers through my hair. *Well Grace, it's big.* He leans back and looks at me, but cannot hold my gaze. He flips through his keys with one hand and Thomas sleeps on his steady arm. I take them, silently, and swing open the front door.

*L*esson *T*hree

The old original sin was chiefly a sin of knowledge; the
new original sin, if I may speak in these terms, is first
and foremost a sin of non-acknowledgement—a refusal
to acknowledge the truth and the laws that proceed
therefrom, laws that we have called fundamental.

Igor Stravinsky
The Poetics of Music in the Form of Six Lessons

After the canvas shades come off the front porch, the house looks lighter, steadier, occupied. We open the windows, air out the spacious, mildewed rooms. The hardwood floors have been refinished recently, the living-room repapered, and one small bedroom upstairs painted a deep, cobalt blue. The kitchen has an icebox and a heavy iron sink, but the plumbing is new, and power lines run from the right corner of the house to our private line of wires and poles that extends out the drive to the main road and into the city of Slidell, population 5870. Thomas sleeps in a wicker basket in the shade of the porch awning and we scrub the kitchen floor and counters, sweep the long empty rooms, peel the faded wallpaper and paint the walls off-white, Rose of Sharon, Camellia, and Montrose. On the third afternoon we drive across Route 11 into the city of New Orleans, walk up West Esplanade Street and into Macy's for curtains, bed sheets, hand towels, slipcovers, one long oriental carpet for the front hall, two small throw rugs for the bathroom, and a General Electric refrigerator in stainless steel with pullout bottom freezer.

Charlie tells me we could never have a house this nice in New Orleans, not on his salary. I fold linen for the upstairs closet. Downstairs, the baby cries and Charlie smiles at me and goes to comfort him. I know, too, he could not have me in New Orleans if he's going to keep another woman like before. I'm safe across Lake Pontchartrain, in Slidell, down our private drive and in our own bayou, surrounded by water, algae, alligators, humidity.

Charlie leaves for work, says, *you know the telephone's working, so if you have any problems, call me. I'll be in my office all day, well, except I guess for lunch, but otherwise, all day, and you can call me whenever you want, it's a private office, Grace, so feel free, that is, if there's any trouble.* I hold Thomas across my shoulder and he cries, louder, drowning Charlie's words in wails. *Ok, Charlie, I'll be fine. You're gonna be late.* I listen to him walk across the porch and down the stairs, then listen to the Chrysler turn over and roar alive.

After I feed the baby, he sleeps in the living-room and I climb the stairs to the blue room. I pick up the violin. I turn it back and forth in my hands, watching the sunlight through the windows reflect on the polished maple and force patterns across the blue walls, the floor, the pale ceiling where the light catches on a metal handle and I see the small, rectangular outline of the door to the attic. I put the violin back on the couch, pull a chair into the room from the master bedroom, climb up on it and pull down the handle, releasing the built-in stairs and an explosion of dust.

I pull my skirt above my knees and hold it there with one hand, use the other to hold myself against the stairs as I climb. Just before I step up into the darkness of the attic, I listen again for Thomas, hear him cry once, wait, hear no more. I continue. I step tentatively onto the wood floor, hoping nothing has rotted too much to hold me. Light muffles through small windows on either end of the attic, and the ceiling slants to the floor along both sides. I walk toward a dark outline near the far window, but find only the broken rungs and brittle seats of kitchen chairs, a gutted sofa ripped and mildewed, and on the ground, among piles of upholstery, ripped shirts and cleaning rags, a small leather case. I pick it up, brush the dust from the stiff and rotted leather, carry it with me back down the stairs, into the light.

The top of the leather cylinder opens with a snap, and inside I find the dull metal pieces of a music stand, the hollow down tube, the adjustable feet, the hinged and flat arms on top. I wipe each piece on my skirt and fit them together, adjusting the stand to my height. I open a book of sonatas on the stand, place it near the window where the light hits each note, each half and quarter, each accent and flat. I put the violin back in its case, loosen the butter hair of the bow, then push the stairs back into the attic and shut the door. The dust drifts down around me, covering my shoulders and hair and I shake my head like a dog after a bath, dust drifting through the rectangles of sunlight and onto the hardwood floor.

New Orleans is a city of walking. Mornings after Charlie leaves, I walk Thomas down our drive, follow the power lines onto Fremeaux Avenue, wait for the bus into the centre of town. There, I wait again for the bus that goes across Lake Pontchartrain on Route 11, meets Route 10 in New Orleans, to St Bernard Avenue, to North Rampart Street, to the corner of Esplanade where it stops and I step off into the heat of the city, to the humidity, where Thomas cries and I hush him against my chest and walk into the French Quarter, to Canal Street, to the Mississippi River.

All the time, the music plays softly back into my head. Concerto in A minor, *This song is a train song,* Concerto for Two Violins, *Here comes the freedom train,* Le Sacre du Printemps, *Just like a Paul Revere,* Concerto for Four Violins and Cello in B minor, *It's coming into your hometown,* The Adoration of the Earth, *Say it loud,* Bing Crosby and the Andrews Sisters, *Riding on the freedom train,* the baby cries and again I hush him, *You'd better hurry* the music lowers behind his wails, then haltingly, *You'd better hurry* unnatural stops and rests, *You'd better hurry* comes back between his sobs, *You'd better hurry* in rhythm with my footsteps. *You'd better hurry down.*

28 May 1948
Slidell, Louisiana

Charlie comes home talking about streetcars, *have you taken them yet, Grace? Nothing like 'em! The advertisements on the sides, the way they move through the city, the cables.* I feed Thomas and he says, *smells good in here, Grace, hey, you've gotta ride these streetcars, and this is what I do all day.* He walks over to me and kisses my forehead, but I know he's thinking about steam and steel, about the lines of track running down each street, about the cables roped above everyone's head, leading. *All day, make sure everything's running smoothly, make sure we've got the best cars in the best places, the right ads for the right quarters, the jewelry for the Garden District, the dry goods for the market.*

I stand up, walk from the living-room into the kitchen and Charlie follows me. *So what did you do today?* and I look at him, his face finally still, his lips parted over his teeth, halfway between speaking and waiting for me to speak. I touch his cheek and then press against him, press my lips against his lips, run my hand slowly down his spine. I hear the music coming back, forcing itself between us, The Ride of the Valkyries, L'Arlesienne Suite, scale progressions and position changes and I pull away, then kiss again without thought, then pull away and Thomas cries.

Next morning Charlie wakes me quietly, before the heat slows us, before Thomas opens his eyes, opens his mouth, before the music comes. We are soft and careful after so much time apart, and still the chords begin, the four-beat measures quickening to a gallop, him moving into me in eighth notes, in long strides then breaking, we move away and I sleep again. When I wake, he is gone, the heat falls heavily across the sheets, across the floor, and Thomas moves in the next room.

I open the windows in the blue room, pull back the indigo drapes. The sunlight folds across the floor, catches the faux leather of the violin case on the couch. I open the clasps, pull out the instrument, tighten the bow. I walk to the music stand and stare at the notes on the page, small black flecks in the endlessness of heat, humidity. I hold the violin by its neck and put the bow in the same hand, push back loose hair from my forehead and feel the sweat there, already at this early hour. Downstairs, Thomas sleeps, and outside, the dust just settles from the Chrysler, Charlie driving too fast out our drive after waking me early and leaving late. I put the bow on the strings and play softly each open string, tuning them against themselves, adjusting the stiff pegs, using the fine tuner for the E-string, playing a D major scale, playing an E minor scale, playing the opening measures of Symphony #7 in A, hear Ortenberg's voice saying, *never mute what should be heard,* move toward the window and listen to the notes erupt into the still bayou, the heat lying heavy across the violin, across the strings, across my temples and down my back where sweat damps my dress.

Charlie came home with a baby pram so today I push Thomas
into the French Quarter and up to the water. I watch the barges
come down the muddy river carting rusted frames, equipment
for the St Bernard gas companies. I push the pram along the
walkway past the Bienville Street wharf, past the Toulouse
Street wharf, to Decatur Street, to the crowds of the French
Market. I push the pram into the market where people handle
the rows of oranges, grapefruit, apples, kiwi, turning each over
in their hands for ripeness, for bruises. I walk past the fish,
their eyes dull disks against the ice, past the pink of sliced
salmon, past the rich scent of gumbo, past the heavy taste of
coffee. I weigh down the pram with two pounds of peaches,
fresh butter, ten russet potatoes. I walk outside between buildings and the sunlight draws sweat in beads across my forehead
where it slowly runs and gathers in my hairline. Thomas is quiet
when I enter the cool of Le Halle des Boucheries for meat, for
the release of the refrigeration and chill of ice. Voices rise
around me calling out prices, arguing about weight, asking for
a thinner slice or a leaner cut. I walk past whole chickens
hanging by their sallow feet, past thick cuts of beef and ham,
past the bloodstained gloves of the merchants.

At Rossi Bros Butchers, I wait behind a woman with three
children and three packages of produce under her thin, tan
arms. She herds the children after the butcher silences each of
them with a piece of smoked turkey. I step up to the glass case
and point to a roast, ask for three-quarters of a pound. The
butcher reaches his gloved hand around the slab of meat, brings
it to the slicer, and then stops. He looks at me, his face gaunt,

his nose pronounced and hooked, his eyes pale blue and deep set. He smiles, pulling his thin lips away from perfectly white, perfectly straight teeth. I smile back, then look away. He turns away, his thin shoulders small points under the bare cotton of his shirt. I watch them move rhythmically as he moves the roast across the slicer. His hair, coarse honey, falls forward across his bent forehead and when he stands straight again he shakes it back from his face with a movement clearly unconscious and often practised. He wraps the meat in a piece of newsprint, and asks if I would like anything else. *No, thank you, that's all,* I say, and he says, *you're not from Louisiana.* It's not a question, and I only nod. He looks at me for a moment longer, hesitates, then turns, pulls off a glove to get my change. He reaches over the glass counter and before I take the coins, I wipe a line of sweat from my face. It's cool in the meat market. His hands, under the bloodstained gloves, are long and fine, though the skin is coarse. I turn quickly away from him after he gives me the change, walk down the aisle between ham hocks, pork loin, plump Cornish game hens lined against the ice. When I look down at Thomas, I feel the sweat drip off my forehead, feel a chill at the cool of the market and the fever of my skin.

When we reach the corner of Esplanade and North Rampart, I'm sweating in earnest, my hair dark around my face and Thomas crying at the suffocating heat, though he has the shade of the pram at least. I hold him under my left arm when the bus arrives, try to lift out the packages with my right, then fold the pram. Passengers climb up the four stairs and I'm the last one, left standing on the cobbled walk while the driver looks on. I want to silence the baby's screams so the music could come back, and it does come back, between the wails, when I set the peaches and butter and roast wrapped in newsprint on the street, fold the pram into tight order and carry all of it under my free arm, the notes play in my head as if I'm reading from the music on the stand in the blue room, lit by the same sun but softer, filtered through the sweet gum and cypress trees, through the palms. The baby cries softly now, and I lean back against the cool of the seat and imagine bowing, moving my left hand across the strings, imagine the soft sound of arpeggio, crescendo, and at a rest, when I close my eyes to the endless flat expanse of marsh and water as we cross Lake Pontchartrain, I see his face, thin, sucked in at his cheeks, his eyes watered like the overcast lake, his hands long, fine, lined and worn from work, I force myself awake again.

The river moves with a slow drawl like the language here, like the voices in the French Market: German, Italian, French, an Irish lilt. I watch the slow crawl of a barge carrying curled cylinders of metal, rusted like the water, mud brown and edged a lighter shade like the scroll of a violin, useless and beautiful in its symmetry. I think of the violin, imagine the workshop, the bench where it rests, gutted, the back removed and elsewhere, the fingerboard split from the belly at its heel and left attached to the curling scroll, the pegs removed, the f-holes opening to air and light and silence.

Charlie tells me again that this will be a great party, that I should look my best, do my hair, *you'll have a great time, Grace, you'll get to meet some people, you can meet my boss, you can meet Arnaut and Benedict,* and I think we haven't been out together since we were teenagers, before Thomas, before we were married, before Philadelphia. I think of Charlie in a suit before our wedding, think what mistakes we've made and think, no, I cannot think that, anyone can say such things.

Charlie says he dropped Thomas off at the sitter's, said the woman seemed lovely, yells up the stairs to me, *she had about ten other kids there, Grace, all yelling and having a great time, I think he'll be fine.* I pin back another loop of butter-coloured hair, freshly washed and dried quickly in the late afternoon sunlight, though still damp from humidity and the sweat that already wants to come. I touch mascara to my eyes and add colour to my lips, then walk downstairs where Charlie takes my hand and whispers, *you look lovely.*

In the Chrysler, Charlie turns on the radio, tells me I can pick a station, so I turn the dial, the music coming back to me, I hear Vivaldi's Concerto in F for Three Violins, hear a slow jazz number, switch to some big band, watch Charlie's fingers tap on the steering wheel and leave it there. *This song is a train song.*

We walk along the cobbled street to house 410, see the coloured lights strung from the windows to the ground, the soft shadows of bodies inside, the rise of alcohol and music lifting into the cool evening air, the darkness closing in. Charlie leads me by the elbow to the front door, rings the bell and when a woman answers, he embraces her then introduces me, and she embraces me as well, her hoop earrings grazing my shoulder, her bare shoulders cool under my fingers, her gloved fingers run across my back. Her back, when she turns to lead us into the house, is bare to the small tip at the base of her spine where the gossamer threaded dress clings gently. Inside, the musicians, a trombonist, a bassist, a drummer, a trumpeter, stand in the far corner of the immense living-room, play blues. Couples dance, drink, Charlie leads me to a second room, finds a short, unshaven man and introduces him, *my boss Mellot, Mellot, my lovely wife,* gets me a mint julep from the makeshift bar in the kitchen, puts his arm across my waist and kisses me, once full on the lips and I feel the blood rush to my cheeks, feel my ears turning hot, then he turns away and walks back to the music, to the women.

Mellot says, *Charlie's a great manager, you know that? Your husband's great at what he does,* and I say, *oh, what is it that he does?* and Mellot hangs his mouth open, his teeth crooked and stained dull grey from smoking, then sucks his lips into a smile and says, *oh, well you know, he manages things. The cable cars, keeps them running, paperwork, you know,* and I smile, *oh yes, I see,* and turn away from him and walk into the larger room where couples dance closely, where a younger man, dark eyed dark haired, leans against an end table and brings a martini elegantly to his lips, where my husband touches the small of the back of a woman, not myself, and I see him as I never see him, separate, angular face clean-shaven, lips full, already richly tanned from Southern sun, his hair, chestnut, now bleached blond in streaks and red where the strings of lights catch it. I watch a woman move closer, touch his arm and laugh, watch her bring a glass to her blood-red lips and tilt up her chin, watch the liquid gather and slide down her long, pale throat and watch Charlie touch back. The music comes back, I hear a melody, quiet and distant under the faster jazz the quartet plays, hear the sickening low moan of Brahms Lullaby on violin, can see the dull play of light across the maple and the oak, the rosewood, can see the red and green and blue lights dull spots on the varnish, can see him touch her back again but feel only the melody moving through me. There is nothing else.

The man with dark features still leans against the end table, alone, and when I look to him I catch his eye as he looks away from me. I walk over, turning the cool glass around and around in my hands. He says hello, he says his name. I give him mine and he takes my left hand from the sweating glass, lifts it formally, to his lips. He lets go of me and smiles, then says, *I see you are married.* I look back at Charlie, see him run his right hand down the woman's spine, his left held still and deep inside his pocket.

I push Thomas through the French Market again this week, and though I know I need to buy produce, need celery, apples, need oranges and lemons, I cannot stop myself from pushing through the crowds, past the housekeepers making purchases for the houses they tend, through the old women who walk slowly and lamely, through the wide and open aisles of the fruit market and the vegetable stands to the sunlight between the buildings and then into the cool damp of Le Halle des Boucheries, to the deep scent of roast and gumbo, through the shouting voices, through the crowds here, more housekeepers, old men smoking cigars and young boys running between legs with packages, a black-and-white dog sleeping in the mud under a display of ice and chicken. I keep walking until I can see Rossi Bros in the distance, the high glass cases lined with different cuts of meat, behind, the stainless-steel refrigerators, the butchers leaning over the counter with the folded newsprint in squares, the glint of sunlight off change. And him. He is taller, thinner than I remember and when I see him, frail under a stained butcher's apron, a thin cotton shirt with the top buttons left open exposing a long, pale neck, I know this is why the rush, this is why I ignore Thomas's cries.

I push the pram sideways against the glass case and look at the different cuts of meat, look up when I realize he doesn't yet see me, see him in profile when he leans across to pass off a purchase, the long face, the hollows at his cheeks, his eyes, so light and watered deep into his face, the Adam's apple that moves up and down in his long, thin neck when he thanks a customer.

When he looks over at me, I look down quickly, but see he is startled, momentarily, that he recognizes me but doesn't remember. Thomas cries and I lean over the pram and hush him, then look up again at the butcher, say, *good morning, I'd like half a pound of turkey breast,* and he smiles at me and when he turns, I see his face shorten in a laugh, or what must be a laugh, though there's nothing to laugh at. He slices the turkey and again I watch his shoulders under his thin shirt, the movement of his arms, the sleeves rolled up to his biceps, the turn of muscle and vein under his pale forearm, the hands, covered in gloves. When he hands me the wrapped package he says, *I'm Henri Rossi,* with a French accent on Henri, and an Italian on Rossi. I laugh this time, and he smiles at me. *And you are?* Startled, I look around, realize that the other customers are not aware of our exchange, I say, *Grace Wright, pleased to meet you,* and I move to hold out my hand, but the glass case is high and I feel awkward and Henri starts to remove his gloves then stops when he realizes I can't reach. We both smile again, and I say *um … could I have some …* but I cannot remember what it is I need to make.

I push Thomas back out of the market, into the suddenness of sunlight, and we walk along the river, watching its slow curl through the city. I hear footsteps coming down the promenade behind me at a run, and then slow to a walk before reaching me. I slow too, turn, and he's there, suddenly shy, uncertain of whether he should speak or not. I smile. We fall into stride together and he says, *I guess you're not used to your local butcher*

chasing after you. They probably don't do that on the east coast, do they? And where on the east coast might you be from? And so I tell him, and we walk, and I tell him more and we are walking in cadence, our footfalls like snowfall, the pram's glide like the slow slide of a trombone or the pianissimo at the end of a song, long, long, till nightfall.

Charlie comes home to my playing, and when I hear the front door creak open, feel the house shudder with the vacuum of humid summer air and coming storm, I put down the bow, brush the sweat from my face and tie back my hair, walk downstairs to greet him. He leans over Thomas, and Thomas giggles and grabs for his hands with his small, fat fingers, kicks like he kicked in my womb at the sound of the violin, at the heat and pressure of heat. Charlie smiles at me and I smile at him. He asks about my day, I ask about his. We have fallen into this. We will not go back and still the music comes back, comes rising through the low-lit room, the strings of lights, the women in their low-cut dresses, Charlie's hands across their backs, his clean-cut face, his laughter, cuts through the jazz and blues he listens to, the big band from up North, cuts through the tight feeling under my eyes, the stifling heat and brings me to a snow fall, the endlessness of space never occupied by anyone, the voice of the violin ringing into the tight, chill air, the strings popping with the cold, Charlie going elsewhere.

I sit with Henri and he rocks the pram back and forth in front of us, keeping Thomas quiet, moving with a quiet rhythm. He asks about my music, about my husband. We have fallen into this, the tessitura, the way we work our lives together, knowing each other without making explicit our tone, our gestures. Here my own music fades back to our music, my fingers lower from the imaginary strings. I watch his mouth move, listen to the song of his words, start to give, just slightly, still look away.

$L^{esson}_F{}^{our}$

To proceed by elimination—to know how to discard as
the gambler says, that is the great technique of selection.
And here again we find the search for the One out of
the Many to which we referred in our second lesson.

Igor Stravinsky
The Poetics of Music in the Form of Six Lessons

I push Thomas down Esplanade Street every day and every day I think about the one I know Charlie has here, black, her arms heavy as sacks of meal, her hands two fists I picture beating dough and rolling it out, then beating again. Must be she holds Charlie under her like that, dark under her like I would be under him in the morning, those few mornings he still wakes me and softly, but she wouldn't be so gentle, must not be. Wonder too, if she knows I walk by with his child, wonder too, if she has a child of her own, or his. The heat beats down on us and even with the thin cotton of a sundress, even with only the small shorts the baby wears he's shiny with sweat and I brush my hair back from my forehead, darkened strands made heavy with salt.

I walk Thomas toward the river where I know I will run into Henri, it's nearly noon and he'll take his lunch, slices of turkey or ham on a piece of rye bread he'll buy at the baked goods stand in the produce section of the market, he'll sit along the edge of the water where it laps under the walkway with a hollow sound, carrying day-old newspaper and the greasy disposed bottles from the night walkers. I can walk by and be surprised by him and he can be surprised by me and Charlie will walk to Esplanade for the woman there, or to Washington Square or Union, or to Iberville or Chartres. We will talk; I will hear the music, try not to listen.

The river sinks slowly across the city, dividing it so I never cross to the south, but forever wander the blocks of the French Quarter, City Park, the Garden District. I remain a tourist in my own city. The low wall that hides the river from the streets holds Henri and I walk toward him, pushing the pram. He doesn't see me. This is the only time I can look at him, from a distance, when he doesn't know. When he sees me he waves, rises from the wall and jumps to the ground, walking with long steps and his head bent down toward Thomas. He speaks to him when he's close, then speaks to me, and I look down, then he looks down when I look at him. Neither of us reaches out to the other, but after this we walk to the wall and he sits again and I climb up next to him and sit, and Thomas sleeps in the half shade of his pram, behind us.

We watch barges pass on the coffee-coloured water. Henri asks about Charlie, about the violin. *Do you know if there's anyone new?* I don't look at him to answer, but watch the dull rust sides of a steamer leave a muddy wake across the river, slowly slowly upstream. *There's always someone new. I don't even know who anymore, try to keep track, but I don't know.* I shake my head, then look at Henri. He looks at me, and it is a moment before we blink at the sunlight, turn away again. *But it doesn't matter.* He sets his mouth and looks across the river, to the low buildings and industry on the farther shore. Quietly, I lay my cheek against his shoulder, only pressing into him in this one, small spot, only touching with the tight skin over cheekbone. And quietly, he runs his fingers through my hair, warmed and softened from the sunlight. I raise my head, look back to Thomas, think, each movement toward him is one of desperation. *I have to get going. I'll see you tomorrow, probably.* He nods, and I swing my legs back over the wall and drop carefully to the walkway, push the pram back to Decatur, to Ursulines, to the corner of North Rampart and Esplanade where I wait for the bus and hear, softly coming back into my head, Bach's Unaccompanied Cello Suites, see through my darkness a player seated before the instrument, his bow wrenching sound from the strings and body, the rosin dancing from the bow, the player dropping his face to the warmth of my hair.

In the light and air I feel the sudden silence of a world without music, I feel the stillness of the Mississippi, of the barge that rests across from me, of the people who walk lazily along the river, I feel the stillness of a silence like that after giving birth, my voice shut to the world and its voice lost to me. I look up from the water and see him, walking toward the river wall with his lunch like he did in '48, in '52, like he still did the last I spoke to him in Slidell, when I last made a choice, chose sound over our gestures.

He sees me watching him, but doesn't recognize me until he is close, then stops and asks, *how did Camille treat you? Everyone alright?* I nod but can barely force a whisper, *yes, Henri, everyone's fine.* He walks to me, takes my arm and leads me along the river, understands that everything has become quiet for me. He says, *yeah, we made it too, course you'd expect that, we're from this city, we know how to handle a little weather, unlike you Yankees.* I smile and relax a little and say, *he left me. Finally. He did it.*

Thomas sleeps downstairs. A cool breeze moves through the opened windows, though still a sweat rises across my skin as soon as I wake in the morning, stays there until I fall to sleep and lose myself in dreams of snow, the frozen lake, the violin swaying in a winter gale, the snow blowing sideways against it and beading across the wood. In the morning, the sweat beads across my forehead. I wipe it now with my wrist, bring the bow back again to the strings, my arm aches from the repetition. Each note comes again and again, I have memorized this violin, myself.

Thomas stays with the woman in Slidell, she's teaching him to speak with a drawl like a violin bow across strings, slow, cadenced. I walk through the city and count the blocks between myself and the market, I know he's there and I want only to touch his skin, to feel the pulse of blood in a wrist, separate from the beat of music through a score, to feel movement different than my movement, than the vibration of horsehair across gut, across empty expanses of humid air.

I enter Le Halle des Boucheries, to the cool of the ice and the dripping water that pools under each stand, to Henri's stand where he sees me and I know he sees me but he doesn't acknowledge this until after the other customers have gone. Then he turns to his brother and tells him he'll return, steps off the platform and walks out with me, silent into the darkening afternoon, into the cloud cover and the air. We walk to the river without speaking, our feet moving in rhythm. I hear Brahms' 5th in my head, hear it to the rhythm of our gait, want to step out of beat, to move away from this noise, measure upon measure, to choose.

At the water, we stop. He says, *Grace ... will you let me hear you play?* And I cannot look at him, see only the arch and hips of the violin, see only my fingers moving across the ebony board, see the peg box, and farther, the useless scroll, turning into itself again and again. I shake my head.

Charlie comes home and tells me he's found a more efficient

route for the 32nd line, says he'll save the company thousands after he's minimized each route, says this as he takes off his shoes and leans back in the chair. Thomas cries, I pour the milk I've heated from the teapot into a bottle and bring it to him, and Charlie says, *do you want to take lessons again, for the violin?* I look up, still holding the bottle for Thomas, his fingers reaching around the curved glass and sliding off again, his mouth moving. *No, Charlie.* I shake my head and look down again. *No, I need something more.* He looks at me without question.

In early afternoon I walk Thomas to the sitter's house and return to our empty rooms, to the silence of the still bayou, of the heat. For four hours, I have this silence to fill without the crying child, without Charlie, four hours until he pulls up the drive, following the electrical wires, leading him like cables lead a streetcar, home.

I walk up the stairs to the blue room. I open the violin case and bring the instrument to my chin, I hold the bow over the strings and look out the window, the drapes pulled wide and the glass opened outward, the two long panels beckoning out like arms, embracing the heat, the hum of insects, the still of algid water and cypress trees. Before I play I listen to the unnatural stillness, lean forward out the window and look up at the sky, the uniform grey where I imagine clouds quickly roll. I come back to the violin, I think of the phone, in the kitchen downstairs, think that Henri might call today, could call and could visit and think I should stop playing so I can hear the ring of the telephone, think the noise will be too great and

I'll miss him and will not see him until next week when I walk back through the market, or stop by the river on his lunch break, or when I call him and ask to meet somewhere, to tell him Charlie didn't come home again last night and that Thomas cries whenever he's not there and so I didn't sleep and that I want to play and play. I draw the bow across the strings, then back more quickly, up a scale and then quickly, the notes forcing movement into the still still air outside the window, the tree branches waving with the vibrato, the static water rippling to a staccato, the long grasses of the bayou dancing down to the water and up to the house, the distant growl of thunder and the soft rain rising and rising and rising to a crescendo that silences the violin, that moves the stately arms of the palm that flattens the grasses that disrupts the solid surface of the water so I put down the violin and run to the window, pull it shut. In the sudden absence of sound hear its ringing ringing.

Charlie wakes me and I wonder if he thinks of another now when he moves across me, brushing skin, softer, then more quickly with a force I cannot hold silently. I think of a B, held in a low sorrow, vibrato like tears, and then think of Henri, close my eyes to Charlie and see Henri's long hands, see the pale skin of his chest, run my fingers down his ribs, run my fingers along the ribs of the violin, the wood varnished so each grain becomes clear, his skin tight across each so each becomes clear when he breathes heavily, his mouth against my mouth, the notes sustained, when I wake Charlie has gone and Thomas cries.

Charlie comes home tonight. He says, *there was an accident today, some stupid kid ran in front of one of the cars, what a nightmare.* He comes close to me and puts his arms around my arms and I recognize a defeat, he still needs. I put my arms across his shoulders, pull him closer to me and work my fingers across the muscle and down the bone of his spine. But I think of moving my hands across him, of the words I should say to him, of what he needs from me and I know I cannot say or do without first making illegitimate each motion and sense. Thomas cries in the next room and we do not move from this embrace. I listen to his breathing, to the heavy intake and his slow control of it when he exhales and I think of the ground underneath us, the cool damp of evening underneath both our backs and of talking, of words I wanted him to hear me say, of wanting to give him a sound or a breath and take his sound and breath and Charlie says, *killed him. Right there, the cable car killed him, wasn't anything my driver could do, I swear it,* and I hush him, keep my arms across his shoulders but already I know I've lost any feeling I had and the music comes back, rushes back overtaking Charlie's voice, overtaking the press of his body against my body.

Thomas went to the sitter's again today and instead I can walk alone through the city, past the jazz houses, past the coffee sellers, past the fortune tellers, past the docks where they drag the fishing nets wet across the planks and pavement. I pass house 410, see the lights still strung across the doorway, hung inside on the upper floors, hung across the rooftop, see the lights fading, blue and red and yellow, inside the house, to the depths where I could see Charlie and the woman with the earrings, see our car parked a block later and touch the wood-grained side, unlatch the back hatch and then press it closed again with a soft click, walk on again to the French Market, to the cool interior of Le Halle des Boucheries, to the scent of cooking and just beyond the Mississippi, ever-moving.

Henri says, *come walk with me,* and we walk across Decatur and down Dumaine, cross onto Chartres and walk toward Canal Street, past the squat brick houses lined in rows, the columns holding their porches upright, the garrets above with green-shuttered windows, closed to the afternoon heat. Past Marie Laveau's House of Voodoo, past flags and flowers, past a white-washed tram, the sound of the donkey's shod feet echoing long after he'd passed. Henri doesn't say anything and as we walk I fight back the feel of violin strings under my fingers, the sound of Le Sacre du Printemps starting over and over in my head.

Chartres ends abruptly at Canal and Henri says, *where do you want to walk?* and I see a cable car slowly moving from a platform, see the driver, his cap pulled down over his eyes, the sun off the flat windshield, say, *I've gotta get home, Henri,* Le Sacre du Printemps frantic in my head, *it's getting late, Charlie'll be home soon and I need to get home first,* the music beating incessantly and Henri says nothing but turns around and we walk back toward Esplanade, North Rampart, the bus, Lake Pontchartrain, Slidell.

Pale dust rises behind me when I walk up our drive. When I look back to where I've come from my movement has obstructed my view and there's nothing left but an emptiness, filling softly with dust and the choke of humidity. I know Henri will not wait. When I enter the house I walk to the blue room, pick up the violin, then place it back again. Downstairs, I pick up the phone, dial Henri's number for the first time. He answers and I say, *Henri I'm so sorry. I'm so sorry.*

Charlie finds an announcement for the Slidell Community and Youth Orchestra and says, *Grace, why don't we go to the orchestra tomorrow night? Maybe it's something you could do.* I look at the ad over his shoulder and Thomas yells, *Mommy!* and I say, *perhaps, Charlie, who knows. Maybe when Thomas is away at school.* Charlie says *tomorrow night, though, we're gonna go, alrighty? Call the sitter.*

Charlie drives to the Slidell Municipal Auditorium after we drop off Thomas at Josephine's house. We walk inside and sit in the middle, four rows behind a blonde woman with a large blue hat and fake pansies in her hair. I see her before Charlie sees her and I know he'll learn her features while I learn the music that they play. When I see her hat catch his eye he puts his hand on my knee and says, *Grace, isn't this exciting?* and I think of high school again, the dusty floorboards of the stage, the violin cold in my hands and my fingers stiff against the strings, I think of the bodies around me, arms moving in and out of unison, searching for an order. I think of each singular note and then the heat that rose slowly inside my throat at the sound, at the growing notes, reaching a unison, the crescendo of sound, at my singular place holding. *Yes, Charlie, it's really nice.* I reach for his hand.

Charlie drives me to the first practice in the cool of night. The players greet me formally, even the children, and then I'm moved back into silence. They speak in groups about Christmas and New Year's, about the success of their last concert in November, the upcoming season. I am tightening my bow when a short woman walks in and the murmuring conversation lowers. The woman walks to me and says, *hello, I'm Janet Lafayette, I'm the conductor here,* and I stand up to shake her hand. *Grace Wright, pleased to meet you.* She's cold, formal, says, *you're not from around here, are you?* I tell her *Philadelphia* and she nods, then steps to the platform.

Alright everyone! Let's get organized! The clusters of players scatter, pick up their instruments and find their chairs in the arrangement. I stand just to the left, near the violins, and the conductor says to me, *so how well can you play? Can we expect a first violin or a second?* I raise my eyebrows, but offer no word, only shake my head. After the awkwardness of her silence, *I'm not sure, honestly.* She says, *Alright then, sit on the last chair on the outside. Share music with Clara. She'll help you along and later you'll have to play for me so I can find you a seat.* The violin is warm in my hands.

After everyone else packs their instruments into cases or slides them into the lockers at the back of the room, Janet Lafayette walks briskly to me and says, *do you have time to play for me now, or should we do this at a later date?* I say, *oh yes, I can play now,* and she seems pleased, and also annoyed at having to wait longer to finish her night alone at home with a nightcap and Brahms on the turntable, played accurately, to speed, and with a precision only professionals achieve.

I follow her to her office, a small room filled with papers, with scores loosed of their binding and littered across the desk, the floor, across the file cabinets in the corner and in the opposite corner an upright bass, looming over us both. She moves quickly through the mess, says, *find a seat if you'd like, I'll find something for you to play.* She moves pages of music around, reaches what she wants and pulls a stand from next to her desk. *Here you are. Now ... I listened to you play tonight and I think you might be alright. But tell me, how long have you been doing this? And with whom?* I tell her, *I started when I was eleven. In the junior high school with the school's music teacher, then later, on my own for many years and last with Edgar Ortenberg in Philadelphia.* She nods vigorously without looking at me, then says, *play this.* And so I play.

Afterward, Janet Lafayette says, *thank you, that was just fine, I think you'll be in the first violin section. I think I could make you first chair, though Darcy wouldn't be happy with that, but anyway, thank you for playing, for joining us ...* I begin loosening the bow, and I think of Charlie at home with Thomas, playing Uno in the kitchen or in the living-room in front of the fireplace because even Louisiana can be cool, can raise the flesh to goosebumps, can force a chill on the air and freeze the lakes so I can walk across, to space no one has walked, can play where no one will hear and the snow will fall in the still soft air, will bead there, lightly, then more quickly in layers of pale light, will bead and then run together across the varnish and drip down the ribs like sweat in the deep heat of Louisiana night with the bed sheets loose over me and the space empty, empty for sound to fill, empty of body and noise.

I meet him at the river behind the Market and he says only *hey*
with his eyes lowered, his feet in stained tennis shoes. I force a
smile and we lean out over the water, side to side, not looking
at each other, though I know his profile, the slope of nose, the
deep set of the eyes, the hair that falls forward and the quick
way he shakes it back from his face. I know his gaunt frame, the
pointed shoulders, the way his shirt falls close against his skin,
I know the sharpness of his hips, the straight rising spine. I
know without touching or understanding how to know. *Grace*
... he starts, but I stop him, shake my head and look across the
river to the distant bank, to the factories at the edge of the
water, to roof after roof expanding from the banks across the
city that I will never own, never make my own. When I look at
him he doesn't turn to me, he sets his lips and then parts them
again, but doesn't speak. *Henri, you know I'm not gonna leave him.
You know* ... He turns to me. *Is it really him?*

We walk along the river and listen to the water slap under the
docks, catch the oil and trash and slowly beat it back against the
piers, under the walkway, out of view. We turn at Canal Street
and walk down, following the overheard cables for the streetcar, walking in the silence of traffic, of voices rising to a constant
hum, of distant and unrecognized jazz. At Royal, Henri asks me
to follow him and we turn right, then left into a narrow alley,
the backs of buildings, low screen doors with the scent of cooking shrimp, of Creole steaming out, metal garbage cans and

cardboard boxes, dark puddles on the uneven cobblestones. Henri stops at two large wooden doors and I read Rossi Bros in faded white letters across them. *This is our processing and storage,* he says, and unlocks a smaller door with number 34 neatly stencilled above the handle.

The music is silent in me. I watch his shoulders as he walks ahead. It's dark and cooler inside, though the heat still clings to our clothes, to our hair. At a silver door he stops, turns to me, says, *Grace ... you know. I don't have to tell you, you know.* The music comes flooding into my head, Le Sacre du Printemps, the opening notes playing over and over, and instead of Henri's face I see the arms of the conductor, moving us together, moving us forward to the next measure and forward to the rising tempo, to the chaos of sound and the choosing, working through the noise to the music, to the violin singing alone, alone, Henri says, *Grace? Grace please listen to me, I really do.* And I say, *Henri I have to get out of here, I have to go,* and turn, walking quickly, thinking of the slower second movement, of the bows drawing in unison and striking in unison, think of Henri's face as I turned, his shoulders hunched, drawing into himself as my bow draws across the strings, releasing, he holds, releasing into staccato, to the bright sun cutting across the puddles of the alleyway, to the distant sound of a horse and cart on Bourbon Street, the hooves pounding rhythmically, and moving off.

Janet tells us to play a sixteenth note faster, to keep up with the brass, with the tempo they want to set because they are the loudest here and I look at the polished maple of the violin, dulled by the artificial light in the hall and look at the shades of maple across the row, the violins settled against the players' legs, the violas with their bloated bodies, and farther the upright basses like men. The flutes start again and we drag our violins to our faces, pull the notes from the strings and I think I hear the far off moan of a telephone. I play louder, enter the measure.

Charlie isn't home from a late night out in New Orleans and Thomas is at Camp Chittenwell in Alabama. Janet drives me home, says, *Grace, do you think you'd like to take some private lessons with me? You're playing tremendously well. I think there's some talent to utilize. I'd like to work with you.* I thank her for the ride, for the offer, she says, *I'm quite serious. Could we start next week? I can meet you here, if you'd like, if it's easier.* I nod, and step out of the car. The air pulls heavily against me and I feel the weight of the violin in its case pulling me closer to the ground, to the heat of the night. Even as I walk inside, I listen for his ringing, for his voice to come to me over the sound of the music, for his face to come to me in my sleep, over the two grinning f-holes, the spruce belly.

The house is silent and vast, unentered spaces for only myself to fill. I turn on the hall light, turn on the kitchen light.

I walk to the living-room. A breeze moves in through the opened windows and chills the sweat beaded across my forehead. I put the violin down on an armchair and stand in the centre of the room, in the dark of the heavy night, listening to the silence of the house, then listening more closely, listening to the cicadas hollowed into the cypress and gum and oak, listening to the frogs with their high-pitched strain. The room closes in. I turn on a light, walk to the fireplace, pull three pieces of wood from the sling rack, pull a sheet of music from my bag and light a match. The first flame flares then dies in the humid air before it can catch the music. The second lights an edge of the paper, burns up it quickly with a low blue flame, turning the eighth and sixteenth notes, the whole and quarter notes, to ash. The flame crawls to the rough edge of a log, plays at the loose bark and catches briefly, climbing up the skin, growing bolder, then fades when the loose outer fold disintegrates, fades before it can catch the grain and weight of the wood itself, fades into the humidity and noise of the night. I rock back onto my heels, wrap my arms around my knees and stare into the dead hearth. I listen to my breathing, think of the great space around me, the emptiness I cannot fill, the violin wood and varnish in its case. I wipe the sweat from my forehead, wipe across my eyes, feel the rise in my throat, the unrecognizable tenor of loneliness.

*L*esson *F*ive

Some saw the intrinsic reason for Art as the abandonment and disdain of the customs and usages of life ... Others denied art any right to be an end in itself.

Igor Stravinsky
The Poetics of Music in the Form of Six Lessons

Charlie leads me by the elbow through the people at the opening, new gallery on Bourbon Street and Charlie knows the
crowd, keeps introducing me and moving on, introducing and
moving on, a refrain for our evening. He remains restrained
until he feels certain we've spoken to everyone, that I will be
comfortable, and then he moves away and I am left with a last
introduction, like a coda come to finish. Charlie moves away to
find a woman he knows, someone who he *met last week, I've gotta
ask her about a new restaurant I think we should try,* and I think he
left me with the tall, awkward gentleman last because he wants
something concrete to blame, someone, a face to argue over
and I make small talk, push the hair that feathers into my face,
say my name again, tell him about the leaves that are changing
in North Carolina, in West Virginia, in the Appalachian mountains of Virginia, of the snow in Pennsylvania that silences the
landscape, makes mute all distance, brings space to all that was
closed, collects across the face of a violin, drips there, splitting
the wood, breaking into the sound, breaking measure upon
measure against me.

Charlie leaves with a short, overweight singer in stiletto heels.
He gives me the taxi fare for the trip home and I tell him nothing. I drink another mint julep from the bar and return to
another man who wants words, not music, and I talk, not in
words but in music, think of Henri, the silence we've formed
for two years, the answer I gave and his reply with an endless

space and all the measures of rest. I see the curved hips of the violin, the menace of the f-holes, see the gleaming cables of the strings, leading me leading me leading me.

I hail a taxi in the first chill of Louisiana autumn, ride back across Lake Pontchartrain, across Slidell to the whisper of leaves dancing across our drive, to the first drops of rain on the still bayou, pull my sweater tighter across my shoulders and think of Petrushka and practice tomorrow evening, of the lesson with Janet next week, think of opening the case, think of tightening the bow, think of the maddening progression, the common movements, the opening and tightening, the lying across the strings, the movement and sound, and stilling the movement, the lack of sound.

I turn at the end of the drive and watch the tail-lights of the taxi streak red into the distance, watch and think to release my own voice into the night air, to open myself to the trees, their intimate rustling, to the rain that runs along the veins of the palm leaves, to the veins of his long hands when they last gestured, the faint press of his fingers through sun-warmed hair, feel the cool water driving harder and harder against my face, my scalp. I pull off my heels, lose my balance and stumble against the dust and mud of the drive, right myself again and push my palms against my face, walk to a sweet gum tree, think again of his hands, uncertain through my hair, think of my hands certain across the fingerboard, the thin spine of the bow, running there, running, I reach the rough bark of the tree and slam my fist against its solid form until I feel the sting of broken skin, feel the run of blood across my knuckles, feel my own force harming the tendon and muscle and soft flesh across the bones. I stop, feel the sharp and throbbing pain in my hand, bring it to my mouth and taste the salt of blood. I hear rain falling steadily, of its own accord, feel the sharp pain and nothing else uncertain or unforgivable or naïve.

Henri leads me right down Canal Street, doesn't say a word after I tell him about Charlie, just moves more purposely through the crowds of shoppers, holds tighter to my arm. The sweat rises across my face, dampens my back. Henri runs his free hand through his hair, and it hangs limply back against his face, the sweat dripping down his neck. A cable car comes past and I hear its noise, the grinding when it slows to pick up passengers, the whir of the cable leading it ever forward. After four blocks, we turn right on Royal Street, then left into a narrow alley, the backs of buildings, low screen doors, the scent of cooking, of red beans and rice, of spice. The cobbles are uneven here, and water collects where they lower, collects and turns rust red, then deeper mahogany, then black with oil, with mud, with the river washed ashore in the hurricane.

At the two wooden doors Henri stops, the faint white lettering less visible than it was twenty years ago and outside two metal trash cans, their lids tight. He lets go of my arm, reaches into his pocket and pulls out the key.

I hear Janet's car pull up the drive and open the door before she's out. She smiles, and we greet each other with an embrace, her violin case held away from me with her free arm. Inside, I offer her a cup of tea, cookies, and she says, *no no, first the music, Grace!* and I hear in her voice something I find myself losing each day.

We walk upstairs to the blue room, two music stands next to each other, their shoulders touching. We open her score, play through the first violin sections, then the seconds. We stop, laughing at our deliberate augmentation of the accompanying parts, then before playing both parts together I say, *Janet do you ever hate it so much that you can't put it down.* She scrunches up her face at me, *or love it so much that you hate it? Hate it for everything it's become to you?* She looks out the window at the still trees, at their solid trunks.

I don't think I play like you do, Grace. She smiles at me. And ... I don't think I've made my life into anything, so I've not stopped anything with the music.

I shake my head. *No, that can't be what I mean,* I argue, but realize I cannot bear the weight of the violin pressing into my shoulder, my chin pressing into the rest, my fingers pressing into the strings, Charlie pressing into me early mornings before I can think of a chord progression, a sonatina to keep him from me, think of Henri pressing against me or not pressing against me, pressing against another woman along the low wall of the Mississippi, its thick waters sinking lower and lower into the city, think of my bow arm sinking lower and lower with each forced note, think of the silence of a winter bayou, of the flat, quiet water, think of the sound of cicadas overtaking the order and motion of each measure, think of all that I've never left to proceed without order and selection, without measured and illegitimate sound.

I walk to the mailbox with my hair tied back in a bandanna after cleaning, after dusting the furniture upstairs, after vacuuming the carpets in the living-room, airing out the sheets on the line Charlie set up off the front porch. I do this to keep from thinking of it sitting silently in the blue room, to keep from pushing the notes off the page and into the spaces outside the open windows, to keep from pushing myself out of the world measure by measure. I walk to the mailbox and my hair remains cool under the cotton cloth, the sun warms only my cheeks, my bare arms, warms my legs and bare feet as I walk down the dusty drive in the heat.

In the box, two letters. One from Thomas addressed only to me, which I open and read, leaning against the curved top of the mailbox, running my toes through the dry soil at the base of the box and unconsciously digging at the dead stalks of flowers I planted there but never watered or noticed again. I scan Thomas's slanted handwriting, the formality with which he addresses me, *Happy Mother's Day, the headmaster asked all of us to write to our mothers and we have decorated our dorm windows with flowers that the girls cut out.* I snort, then laugh out loud at the idea of shaping construction paper into petals and stamens, of pasting it to the glass of windows, of looking, from a distance, at this absurd indiscretion—a flower sprouting from the emptiness of glass.

I turn to the second letter, in my mother's handwriting, split open the end and begin walking up the drive after I reach down to pull a dried chrysanthemum leaf from between my toes. Again I skim quickly, but stop in the middle of the drive to read back again, slowly, weighing each of my mother's words and holding them past their value, holding them into the silence in which I should feel, and wait for the next note, and feel, and play out this feeling.

Grace, It further saddens me to write to you with such terrible news, but your father died this morning and though I could call to more quickly relay the information, I feel there is no need to rush this progression. You will find out and will not be able to return to Philadelphia for a funeral either way. It was a complication in emergency heart surgery. Like his father, the muscle was not strong, gave out unexpectedly and too soon. He would have liked to do so many things. But this, I suppose, is to be expected.

I imagine my father on a bed under the pale blue of sheets and outside his hospital window children passing a white ball quickly between themselves, their shouts silent gestures and inside the sound of low voices moving to a distant and vacant hum, like the distant whine of the train when I walked down Ridley Creek in daylight, its galloping galloping always far and incomplete.

Charlie comes home early after my phone call and immediately embraces me, pressing my face against his shoulder. After a moment I pull away, tell him, *Charlie, I think I should go up there for the funeral. I think Thomas should come along too, and you, too.* He sees I've not been crying, I am composed and suffered his embrace for form, and for the customs and usages of life. He nods his head, *yes, I think so too. I can get you on a train tonight, get us on a train tonight. We can call the school, but I don't know if they'll*

let us rip him out of a week of classes like that, and really, he didn't know his grandfather very well, what effect will it have on him, really? But his face softens when he looks again at me. *Of course I'll call. He should be at his grandfather's funeral.*

We walk through the woods together, past the collapsing tobacco barn hidden in the overgrown raspberry bushes at the edge of our property, over the stone bridge I would walk each evening after Charlie left, would walk toward the violin that waited in my bedroom for its release. We walked over the soft ground of trails in the state park, maintained and manicured, mulched like garden paths, I tell him, *I walked here every day when I was your age and older, walked here, played here, met your father here and ...* He is silent next to me, looks up respectably when I speak but only nods, then watches his feet again. *I used to bring my violin out here and play sometimes, at night.* This intrigues him, he says, *you play the violin? I had no idea*, his voice holding no trace of the Southern accent we'd hoped to protect him from with a Northern education. *Yes ... yes, I play, I've always played, I play in an orchestra right now, I played when I was pregnant with you.* He purses his lips and then smiles at me, *well I'd like to hear sometime, mother. I've never known, even summers when I'm at home. Had no idea.* I feel the spaces entering me again, spaces no one has filled and then I smile at him, think of the mature voice he has adopted, the astute observations, the language. I say, *hey, let's get away from this trail and walk in the water, ok?* and we take off our shoes and race to the water, to Ridley Creek. He splashes in first and I follow a moment later, the water cold up my legs, my dress held above my knees, each movement suddenly restricted by the pull of the current.

When we reach the middle where the water reaches nearly to his hips, soaks through his wool trousers, he says, *Mom, do you think it's alright that we're doing this? I mean, there's a funeral tomorrow. Is this ... would this be alright ... would your father be alright?* I smile at him and look to the bend in the river and nod my head, *yes, I think so.* And I think this is too much as one would plan it, a walk downstream with a son in celebration of strengthening one relationship at the loss of another and I think, but this is not really strength. The water tugs at my legs and I remember the violin, held high above the current, the maple and spruce dry and light above my shoulder, the motion inky in the first light of morning and cool. A chill runs up my spine. *Hey, let's go back.*

Charlie comes home late and I don't question this, but he enters excited, says, *Grace, I'm gonna get us a new car. Looked at 'em today on the way home and picked one out.* He smiles and I return this smile, feeling nothing but the rise of Vivaldi in my ears. He sits, begins unlacing his boots. *It's a beauty of a car, a Dodge Dart, a little thing, two door, sporty, Grace, really sporty, gonna move like a bullet, V-8 engine. It's an automatic, a 3-speed Torqueflite.* I nod vigorously, uncertain of what to say, knowing I've lost even my ability to pretend. *What colour, Charlie?* and he rises, walks to me and puts his hands on my hips, pulls me toward him as if we'd never been apart, says, *red with a white racing stripe, a real beauty, call it Bing Cherry Red in the catalogue ... but I saw 'er in real life, don't worry, she's lovely. You'll love her.* I think only of silencing the rising music, think of the only mute, the image of Henri's loss when I turned around, the image I've construed, the image I'm no longer sure was close to anything real and for a moment I feel the heat rise in my throat.

I feel the rising notes before I play them, run my fingers up the throat of the violin, up the fingerboard till they stretch to the highest pitch, think if I play frantically enough I can shatter the desire to play at all, think if I lead everyone forward, lead like gut strings down the ebony fingerboard, lead like the cable of a streetcar, I can bring us closer and closer to the collision, closer and closer with each rising pitch, the first violins in strange accord, each note a strain, the seconds playing the shadow harmony, an octave below but always rising, the violas bursting madly from their swollen bodies, the upright bass watching and rising himself and watching. Only the cello holds us with the sorrow and the abandon. Only the cello can bring us to an end, complete within ourselves.

$L^{esson}_{S^{ix}}$

The first condition that must be fulfilled by anyone who aspires to the imposing title of interpreter, is that he be first of all a flawless executant. The secret of perfection lies above all in his consciousness of the law imposed upon him by the work he is performing. And here we are back at the great principle of submission that we have so often invoked in the course of our lessons. This submission demands a flexibility that itself requires, along with technical mastery, a sense of tradition and, commanding the whole, an aristocratic culture that is not merely a question of acquired learning.

Igor Stravinsky
The Poetics of Music in the Form of Six Lessons

I stand in front of the window, the indigo drapes dropped to two piles at my feet and the sunlight unfettered, cutting across the wood floor, angling off the metal of the music stand, catching the varnish of the instrument and warming it in my hands. I stare at the four strings, their progression from the tailpiece to the curling upon themselves in the peg box, looping over and over to the right tension, to a balanced pitch. I turn the bow in my right hand, watching the sun glint off the ivory inlay and tease up the dark walls. Outside, the air is still, the water is quiet, the dust settles in the drive and doesn't rise up again, the leaves on the cypress, sweet gum, on the oak and palm, do not whisper or cast shadow across the ground. The sun rises directly overhead. I think to place the bow across the strings and call a sound into this still bayou and then I hear its distant ringing downstairs.

I take the stairs quickly, still holding the violin. When I reach the receiver I set the bow on the counter, then breathe deeply and feel the line of sweat drawn across my forehead, think what is this that makes me run for the telephone, why today. It rings again and I pick up the receiver. *Hello?* His voice on the other side, tinny, sounding older and not old. *Hi.* The heat rises in my throat and I do not question, think only of the one sound he's uttered, the sustained note of his voice in the air. *Grace ... I've been thinking about you. I would really like to talk to you sometime.* I nod and nod, realize there's no sound coming from me, say, *yes Henri, of course please, yes Henri.*

Nearby the traffic wails across Route 11 and when I step out of the Town and Country and walk toward the door, I see him rising out of a brown car I never knew he drove. I think, so much I've not known. He smiles, and we walk toward each other and then stop a few feet separate, uncertain of where to proceed to, or from. I mumble *hey* and he says the same and then I say, *well, should we get some food?*

We walk to the door that I open, we walk inside and I pick the farthest booth, dark and near the bathrooms, but silent, alone. He folds his tall frame into the plastic seat across from me and looks at the menu. I watch him, his face thinner still but lined now. Before he can look up, I glance down at the menu too, and for several seconds we sit in silence. He pushes his hair away from his face with his fingers, more worn than I'd expected or remembered. I look down again and he says, *I've ... I've really missed you. I don't think—* The waitress leans across our table and says, *what can I get you? Y'all know what you want to drink at least?* I look up at Henri and part my lips, then glance at the woman and say, *please just some water for me.* I need to ease the heat that rises in my throat and threatens to be feeling. *A cup of coffee please,* he tells her and she waddles away, the apron cutting a line over her backside. Henri looks away again, and I say, *yes, of course I've missed you, too. I ... I don't think I even know how much I miss you.*

I put my hand to my forehead and press into my temple, think this is not me speaking, these are not the words I've always wanted to find in myself, to say without the thought first, to sound out like the notes of a piece first played, uncertain because they are not practised, made false. And still I know I am performing, executing. *I don't know,* he says, *I don't even know why I wanted to meet with you again, don't know what*— The waitress brings my water in front of my face with a flourish *and here y'are dear, one glass of water and for you, sir, coffee, made fresh. Now then, what'll it be?* We are silent, look at each other then she looks between us. *Well com'on now, you've gotta be hungry right?* I smile up at her and say, *how about you give us another minute, ok?* And her, *sure enough, can do,* and her waddle once again. He looks at me and I meet his stare, but feel myself hardening inside. He says, *I ... I don't know what there is to say, nothing really, we've said it all, or not said anything at all and don't have to, it's all there.*

He sips on the coffee and I run the edge of the menu under my finger, think I've wanted this for so many years and now, right in front of me, I cannot even begin words, cannot think of anything that isn't already finished before I say it. *Henri ... I ... how are you? Christ, it's been almost eight years ... maybe more than that. What's ... what have you ... how ... I don't know, Henri, this is so*— She leans over our booth once more, *alrighty folks, y'all know yet?* And I look quickly over the menu, say, *just give me some pancakes, ok? maybe something ... some hash browns on the side.* She nods and scribbles on her notepad. *And how many you want, dear? Two, three?* I think of the storage building, the long alley and the uneven cobbles, *two's fine.* The water, dark and with a film of oil that reflected the sun. *And you, sir?* I think of his face, younger, but unchanging, or that I've changed him. *I'll have a waffle, two eggs, over easy.* She pulls the menu from under my hands, forces us to look up at her with her abruptness. *K folks, comin' right up.*

I look at him again, swallow the cold water, think of snow,

of the flat expanses of lake, of the *I've been … I've been fine, I guess. You know. The usual. Not too much changes.* I nod, look at his face, at the way his eyes seem lighter now, less blue than before and nearly a translucent grey, like the lake reflecting the sky from the window of the bus, the packages shoved against the metal wall, the pram folded at my feet, Thomas on my lap. *My brother quit working for us. He moved to Tennessee, the Hatchie Mountains, wanted to see something other than the good ol' muddy Mississippi.* I nod again, think of the rise of mountains in Pennsylvania, their spines gentle into Virginia and West Virginia, into North Carolina and lowering into the warmth, the bayou, the lake and river and gulf. *And you? How've you been?* I look down again. *Oh, well, you know, the same too, I guess. Thomas is finishing up his last year at the Kiski school in Pennsylvania. Took summer classes and wants to go to UVA next fall. I guess he will. My father died a few years ago … and … I'm still—* She leans across with plates of food balanced on a broad forearm, says, *and here you are dear, two pancakes, one side of hashbrowns and for you sir, one waffle, two eggs over easy, you folks need anything else right now, some syrup right here, need some ketchup, anything else?* I shake my head no and Henri says, *not right now, thanks,* and she talks again, says, *well you just let me know, k?* I pick up my fork. *Uh … yeah, I don't know … what … I started playing in an orchestra. That's about all. Nothing to say, really.* Henri cuts into his waffle, breaks the thin skin of the eggs and I watch them bleed into the waffle, bleed into the groove of the plate. *Charlie?* I pour some syrup across my pancakes, listen to the voices of men at the counter, their drawl faint in the background next to the whine of the highway. I nod slowly, look up at Henri. *The same.*

When the waitress returns we're silent, eating more quickly

than necessary and she is silent as well, looks across our table, meets my eye and nods, then walks back to the kitchen. Henri says, *you know…it would work out. It could.* And I look up, think I've had this conversation before, or react like I have, think I've felt this and catalogued the feeling and can pull it up, like I use a scale to warm up, always there, waiting, I say, *yes. Yes, I know, but it won't. We both know.*

I enter the blue room again, the repetition. Removing the violin, tightening the bow, tuning the strings to themselves, tightening the pegs upward. I bring the violin to my shoulder, walk to the window and feel the heat, look at the music on the music stand and know I cannot bear the weight of the instrument any longer, its pressing into my neck and shoulder, its slow movements into me, the curve of the waist and the curling scroll, ever beckoning. I lower the Pernambuco bow then wing it wildly through the air, understanding its fragility, the lack of weight. I drop the violin to my side and tighten my grip against the fingerboard, turn it over and over in my hand, spinning it faster and faster, look out the window at the gum and cypress trees, at the glint of water farther away, the still grey of it, think of the news report that a hurricane grows like a tumour, becoming a fist, tense for the blow. I tighten my fingers to a sharp fist over the fingerboard, drop the bow to the ground and hold the violin with both hands, turning it like a piece of fruit, ripe, waiting to be bruised. All could be silent.

Charlie sits on the couch next to me and we watch the evening news, special edition with a report of the developing hurricane that grew as a tumour, far off the Gulf Coast, farther still to the endless ocean, the expanses of frozen water no one has entered or filled. Charlie drinks a martini, says, *exciting, isn't it? Wouldn't'a had something like this happen in Philly, that's for sure.* I think of the violin swinging in its case, of walking the streets to Ortenberg's, of the office with the children outside, throwing a ball, their white frocks like sun spots, dancing across the walls, the rise and fall of the violin's voice and Ortenberg saying, *you've read the Stravinsky, haven't you? So let's think of a submission to music, of giving in to each note, Grace, making each your note, playing flawlessly because it owns you, not because you have mastered the sound.* Charlie says *listen to this* and I look closely at the anchorman, his face sharp, gaunt, his eyes deep set and light, uncoloured on the fuzzy television screen, his hands folded in front of him but fine, long fingered, pale, he says, *we recommend everyone coastal, Chinchuba to Biloxi Bay, head inland. This looks like the biggest hurricane to hit the coast in the history of the US, folks, so please, head inland, take your pets, the Red Cross is setting up evacuation stations in Baton Rouge and Alexandria, stations have been made available in Hattiesburg Mississippi, in Columbia. Once again, we recommend everyone coastal, Chinchuba to Biloxi Bay, head inland.* Charlie shakes his head, laughs. *No need, no need,* and I watch the anchorman closely, think of Henri's face, the rough-honey hair, the motion of jerking it from his face, from his eyes, his long fingers, rough from work.

He pulls the keys from his pocket, his long fingers flipping through the silver and bronze, his bare forearms pale in the harsh light that slants into the alley, that reflects off the dark puddles among the cobblestones, that burns into my hair. The sweat soaks my back, runs down my breastbone. The heat presses us closer and closer to the cool of the cobbles, to the cool metal door with 34 stencilled neatly over the lock that Henri turns, pushes open. The darkness invites us, the interior damp and musty. Henri shuts the door behind me and we become alone in the dark and silence. I feel him reach for my arm, touch carefully and lead me forward down the hallway. His fingers against my skin are certain, definite. Slowly, his outline becomes clear to me, walking a step ahead and confidently toward the stainless-steel doors that we feel rather than see, feel the sudden and pleasant cool of refrigeration, feel the metal nearly hot against our hot skin.

He says *Grace* but I hush him with a finger to his lips, then press against them, but uncertainly, pull back quickly. He puts a hand on the door to the refrigerator, says, *in summer, we, it's cool in here,* and pulls the door open. Inside, the light is dim, painting everything milky, a shade of blue like that of the lake before a storm, thick with stillness. He closes the door and the chill comes over me, catches the sweat across my back and shoulders, across my forehead, cools me. Henri turns to me, steps in close, says *Grace* but I hush him again, my finger to his lips where it stays, then slowly traces across them, down his cheek, down his neck to his chest where I place my hand. He reaches to my shoulders, his hand sliding to the small of my back. His face is sallow in the light, hollows at his cheeks, his eyes dark in the half dark, set far into his face and his hair is light grey under the water, moves through my fingers like fish through grass, waving with the current, my own breath coming slowly, catching the bit of oxygen left, catching and holding like the final note of a measure, holding into the next, its maple flesh gleaming in the sunlight, smooth under my fingers, its ribs curving into waist, his ribs sharp under the thin shirt then suddenly to the sharp hip and the press of his belt when he steps into me. I see the f-holes, mouths beckoning me to the sound, to the cool inner reaches of the instrument. He puts his lips against my neck, moves up my neck, I move my fingers up its neck, playing across, playing lower, moving softly, my thumb guiding underneath, along the spruce underbelly, the strings leading me closer and closer. He leads me farther into the refrigerator, and we step like dancers, into and away from each other, then back together, dancing like the cypress leaves danced up our drive with the first wind, then halted with rain, halted and blew again into the sides of the house, against the canvas screens, blew upward to the window of the blue room, touched the glass then blew inside when the storm forced the window inward, shattered it across the hardwood floor, pushed over the music stand, spilled the sheet music under the couch, against the drapes, blew rain across the case and then lifted it from the floor, lifted it in a whirl with Petrushka, with Vivaldi's Concerto in D major, with Bach's Concerto for Two Violins, his hands move quickly up my spine, move into my still warm hair, the wind rips the violin from its case and throws it, the strings singing loudly against the wall where it hits, then muting with the rain, becoming heavy, the body filling with water, I gasp in the water-coloured light and he comes closer, runs his hand down my breast, leans in and moves his lips across my neck, says, *Grace, I've wanted* ... then hushes, moves his lips to my lips I see the violin, darkened with water, the useless strings, the dangling tailpiece, his fingers near my mouth, I pull away from him, my hand pressing into his chest, pushing him back, say, *Henri I can't, Henri, no,* think, I would do to him, too, think, no, always the violin. He steps back, runs his hands through my hair, and his face, his face, I think of the crack from the maple back to the base, think of the dull tapping inside, hear the tapping, tapping of a beat, see the swinging bow, the notes long, low, then staccato, rising and rising I step away, their short strokes, mai legato.

I walk up the drive to the front door, alone now. I think of the violin waiting silently for my fingers to caress the notes from the strings. I open the door, walk into the cool of the front hall, up the stairs to the blue room. I look at the white curtains fluttering uncertainly in the sunlight. I move toward the case on the couch, run my fingers over the clasps. It is done, this decision. And then I know when I open the case there will be the space its body should occupy and doesn't, the places his hands could touch and will not, the expanses of wood and ice to fill with a sound and never feeling, the slow falling snow and the creak of sycamore and spruce, the distant rumble of a train, the felt-lined interior, waiting, empty.

Acknowledgments

Thanks to Steven Millhauser for his guidance and reading while writing this book. Thanks also to Kathryn Davis and to Barry Goldensohn for their close reading, as well as to Dom Benincasa and Reed Fischer. Thanks to Sinead Deegan and Martin Rice for their hospitality and support.

I'm forever grateful to the faculty of Skidmore College's English department for their encouragement and instruction.

Finally, my extreme gratitude to my parents and family for all of their support.